T0374193

RED*Velvet*

PG

authorHOUSE®

AuthorHouse™
1663 Liberty Drive
Bloomington, IN 47403
www.authorhouse.com
Phone: 1 (800) 839-8640

Published by AuthorHouse 10/19/2018

ISBN: 978-1-5462-4062-4 (sc)
ISBN: 978-1-5462-4061-7 (e)

Print information available on the last page.

Contents

Chapter *One*

"The wet lands and green lands are always wet and green. Every season has its own beauty. Summer here is heaven on earth. It is a rainbow of colours. It's as if life has reborn again and again. Now winter, that is a whole new look. A look of heaven again, white heaven. It's like living in a dream where everything is asleep yet full of life. Winter has made me realise that my life somehow is not real. it's like a dream and sometimes I feel like I'm living a life of missing parts that don't make sense. I see flashes, I feel and touch things that are not there, but are apart of me. When I'm awake I feel like I'm dreaming and when I'm dreaming, I feel like I'm in another world that does not makes sense. I hope next time I write something again I will be able to see something clearer." She closed her diary with that thought.

As Sharon looked up and watched herself in the mirror, she passed her fingers through her golden hair and smiled with content, because she loved her blonde hair. She lived with her grandparents (father's side). No one but just her lived with them. As she came down the stairs she would hear voices and see flashes inside her head. She saw distinct places, saw things and heard distinct voices as well, "get away from the window dear, daddy you're home". She kept this to herself, not even her grand parents, she never told them.

The village Sharon lived in was small and comfortable. Sharon would not trade that place for anything. It was situated close to the forest. The people who lived there were closely knitted. Everyone knew everyone. They shared each other's happiness and sorrow. Even though the village was small, there were a lot of activities going on. The market place was busiest of all. The men sold their animals, got hair cuts and just hang out. The women did everything you could think of. You could hear their laughter for more than a mile away.

There would be children running up and down, helping their mothers with their products. There were trades from other villages visiting nearby. The men and women folk worked very hard together. The village was full of wealth and the villagers were contented with themselves. The forest helped to provide logs for warmth and to build houses etc.

There were carpenters, masons, wielders, tailors, cooks, craftsmen and gardeners to name a few. There were also learned men who can cure the sick, prevent sicknesses by using mother nature's herbs and bushes. Then there were the swordsmen and wrestlers who enjoyed a little sport now and then. The women assisted their husbands in their work. They took care of the homes and children. No one complained because they all worked in harmony, sharing each others happiness and sorrow.

Sharon gave a sigh of boredom, doing the same things everyday. She understood that her grand parents were over protected but did not protest. In general she lived a very simple but safe life. Her birthday was only a few months away. She would be eighteen. Her grand parents were constantly checking on her birthday which puzzled her a lot. Why her, she thought, but little did Sharon know that her entire existence will change at the age of eighteen. Only fate can decide her future. To her it was just an ordinary day. She dreamt a lot about Prince Phillip, who lived in a castle so very far away. He was the perfect match for her, she thought.

She loved him so, suddenly she came to her senses and realised how stupid she was and smiled with herself and thought it never hurts to daydream about her prince. She found it very strange why she thought about Prince Phillip so much and she has never met him and never will because they live in two different worlds, even though he became part of her life thinking about him so much.

Sharon heard the sound of horses galloping around her. As she turned around, she saw the messenger. "Hello Mr. Fred you are early today." "Yes, I want to take advantage of the whether we are having. Please give this letter to your grandparents." "Yes I will, bye now." Her grandmother snatched the letter from her hand and told her to bring in the animals because it was going to rain later. Sharon noticed that whenever they received a letter from the Shepperds, they became very anxious and send her away."Grandmother, grandfather, why are you so anxious to read this letter and then you will send me away so I will not know of it?

"Oh, don't worry about this dear, it doesn't concern you, This is just for old folks like us, now run along dear." Sharon did as she was told, but hid behind the door and looked on. She saw how they held each other hoping that the letter had no bad news. They both got up and looked at the calender spotting the month of her birthday. She heard the excitement in their voices. She could not understand what her birthday had to do with the letter or the Shepperds. She wanted to speak to them but as always, whenever they got this letter, it's the same old story. She could not get anything out of them. She just did as she was told.

There was still daylight when there were a lot of excitement not too far from her home. The forest was not far from her house. Sharon could hear dogs barking, horses galloping and men shouting. As they came closer, she saw a lot of soldiers and guards scattered in the forest. This brought the attention of the surrounding neighbours. As the soldiers came they ran in all directions looking and shouting, running into the forest searching for something or someone, then left the same way they came. She waited to see or hear anything else, but everything became normal again, everyone went back to their houses and it was normal again.

Every Friday evening, Sharon and her friends would go to the edge of the forest and enjoy an evening of dancing, singing, eating and just hanging out. They loved the beauty of the valley they lived on. There were beautiful flowers, benches to sit and talk and also swings from the large trees. That very evening Sharon saw her grandparents took a carriage and went to the Shepperds. She watched as the carriage passed by. "Sharon to earth," said Lucy, her dear friend.

"What is wrong, you look worried." "It's nothing'"

she said "Well then, let's get back to partying," said Lucy. Sharon smiled and they both hugged each other. The moon was so beautiful, Sharon's hair looked like gold dust across her blue eyes and face. "You know, you look like a princess," said Ralphy, her friend she grew up with. "Right," laughed Sharon. She was indeed very beautiful. "I'm not so sure," said Tom who was passing drinks for everyone with a smile.

"You see if you are a princess there must be a prince somewhere." I'm sure it's not you" answered Ralphy, "your nose is too large." There was laughter. Tom turned around and strangle Ralphy. "I suppose you are the one eh?" answered Tom. "Well if you say so," said Ralphy. There was more laughter. As the sun was rising the pigs, hens, goats made their noises because it was feeding time. Sharon was already up. Her cottage was light blue with red borders around the windows and posts. It had one chimney, with bright flowers in front and around the house. There was a barn at the back of the cottage where the animals were kept. There was a small porch at the front of the cottage with a swing. There Sharon would sit and swayed herself, drank tea and always tried to figure out what those flashes and noises were about.

Rain fell almost the entire afternoon. The weather was a bit foggy and damp. Sharon came inside after attending to the animals. To her surprise, she saw grandmother sobbing very sadly and grandfather trying his best to console her. Sharon ran towards her and asked what was wrong. She put her arms around her and grandmother continued crying. "What is it grandmother?, she asked very concerned, but they both continued to console each other.

"O Sharon, everything is fine, just fine dear," said Alfred, her grandfather. "What is it, I want to know what is going on, tell me," she pleaded to them over and over. "Sharon it's just that I hope it is not lost, then everything will be hopeless." "What did you drop grand mother, tell me, I want to help. "Oh Sharon, my dear Sharon, I hope I find it." "Of course, you will grandmother, I will find it for you. What is it?" You were there only yesterday, we still have time to look for it before any one finds it, what is it?"

There was silence for a while. Sharon had never seen or met the Shepperds. She was not allowed to go there at any cost. Grand mother was too distressed as well as grandfather. "I know that I'm not allowed to go there, but you have to ask yourself, which is more important, not going there or finding what you drop that was so valuable." They thought for a while and decided that she was right. "We will accompany you and direct you dear. It is a compass with green border and a large face." Sharon assured them that she will surely find it. Mr. Smith was the driver of the carriage and also the handy man.

As Sharon drove with them she saw Tom and he waved at her. After a good distance away Mr. Smith took a left turn which was a very narrow dirt road. The road was very wet with potholes. Nobody lived in that road, it was scary and dark. The rain began to fall again with lightning and thunder. "Don't be afraid dear, it's just lightning it will be over soon. Sharon had never seen that part of the valley before, there were very tall trees on both sides of the road. They were covered with, twigs and bushes which makes it difficult to see beyond them. At last Mr. Smith said "woh" to the horses and

Sharon knew they had reached the Shepperds. She was about to jump out when her grandmother held her back and said. "You see those chairs, I think I dropped it there, check there first my darling.

Chapter *Two*

As Sharon came out of the carriage she was astonished to see something she had never seen before in her entire life. Her eyes opened bright and she became spell bound.

What she saw was something like a large hill but when she looked carefully it looked like a very large building covered with trees, bushes and twigs with little entrances that look like windows. At one side of the hill, she saw a very huge arch covered with the forest. What surprised her most was at the front where she was standing the grass was well groomed for almost all around the hill. It was a beautiful sight indeed. The rain had stop falling and Sharon saw the scenery more clearly.

She couldn't speak, just stared. "Sharon hurry now, the chairs at the right of you. "Sharon jerked herself when she heard her grand mother's voice. She saw the tables and chairs. They were white in colour and she headed towards it. "Please find it dear, quickly now." "Yes grandmother," answered Sharon. Sharon looked around the chairs, she felt as if she did this before right here and then. It was so familiar with her. Sharon looked at the table and heard laughter from children, saw biscuits and tea in very shiny and silver cutleries. The table and chairs became brand new she saw a beautiful woman who called out her name, "Sharon, tea is ready let's have some."

She became more puzzled when she saw the pattern and designs on the table set. "This is the design I drew home. How could that be, impossible.

"Sharon, did you find it, the rain is coming again." Sharon began to look on the grass not too far from the tables and chairs but was closer to the hill. "I found it grandmother." Before she left, she turned around and look at the hill and she swore she saw a fountain came to life with beautiful lights around it.

There were children running around it and having a merry time. "Sharon come now, don't waste any time." "Coming grandmother," she said. As she entered the carriage she could have sworn she saw movements in one of the windows. As the carriage went by Sharon bent over and gazed at the hill, the beautiful lawn and tall trees once again.

"Thank you Sharon, I knew you would find it, you are such a wonderful girl. There is nothing you wouldn't do for us." They both hugged. Grandmother I told you everything is going to be all right." After dinner, they decided to go to bed early, because they had a traumatizing day. Before they left Sharon asked to see the compass. "It's just ordinary dear, the important thing is that you found it." "Yes, but I would like to see it because it so important to you." She was hesitant and with a sigh she went to the cupboard and gave the compass to her.

Sharon looked at it and said the glass face was rather big for a compass. "Yes my darling quite true," said Alfred her grandfather. Sharon held it on her hand and began to look at it carefully. "Why is it so important. I thought you would have fainted or something when you thought you lost it, it seems ordinary." "We just didn't want to part with it. This has been in the family for a very long time." Grand mother took the compass and turned to Alfred and said, "you see it is still intact".

The casing is still on without a scratch." "There is a casing?" asked Sharon. "Yes, see for yourself" said grandmother." Sharon looked again at the compass and saw it. "Have you tried removing it? "Don't be silly child," said grand mother and before she could stop her the casing was already out. "I always wanted to know what has a large face with green glitter around it. Then a hand will take it from me and pat me on the head. It is the same compass I'm telling you the truth."

"You must have been mistaken dear," said grandmother. "I've seen this so many times before. I remember wearing a beautiful red dress fit for a princess and I held the compass in my hand." Her grandparents were speechless and Alfred asked. "You said a red dress fit for a princess?" "Yes, yes and in the dream I was so proud to keep the compass because It was given to me for safe keeping." "Oh dear," said Alfred and almost fainted. He grabbed a chair before he could fall. "How did you get this compass, I want to know all about it," she asked.

"Sharon, when did you start dreaming about this compass?" asked grandmother. "Almost everyday and night, I don't know exactly, these dreams and flashes are so jungled up and they don't make sense, but this does, it's real." The grandparents just sat there looking at each other speechless. They were stunned. "Give the compass to me dear, I want to look at it, we will talk about it in the morning and if you dream about it again, let us know." "No, I want to keep it," said Sharon. She closed her eyes. "No, don't do that, open your eyes child," "Grandmother I tell you it is the same compass.

Look there are some letters at the back of it when you hold it diagonally. I know the letters, I will tell you." "Sharon please stop," said Martha. "I know the letters, I will tell you they are K.D.N. check and see for yourself," said Sharon. Sharon opened her eyes and saw her on the floor. She ran towards her and gave her water to drink, then put her to lie on the bed. "Oh Sharon, what have you done, you should have never taken out the casing," said Alfred. How can this be possible, she saw the initials of her father, how can this be," said Martha. "You said something grandmother?" asked Sharon.

Her grandmother mumbled something again and then fell asleep. Sharon was bursting with excitement. "How do I know this engravement.?" She asked herself. "All these years they had it and I did not know, all these years."

The window was opened and the moon was in its glory. It was shining more that night. Sharon looked at it and asked, "how do I know the engravement. I have never seen it before." Her long white robe shuffled against the cool breeze with her hair sparkling as ever in the moonlight. She wondered if the engravement was real, then all the flashes and dreams were also real. They must be real, they must they are real. "Oh I don't understand, maybe some of them, the bed chamber, mother, father my younger brother and sister, the dancing, horseback riding. This is impossible, I am so confused right now.

I can't be a princess with a crown she laughed. My grandparents have a lot of explaining to do in the morning. If the compass is real, then the ring is also real." With that she blew the lamp out and went to bed. During the course of the night, Sharon grandparents whispered in their room. "How long has she seen these flashes. It's a miracle. I thought after what happened the poor child had lost her memory, she was only eight. "She was a very clever and bright child in the kingdom, sweet Sharon, what are we going to do." "We'll have to confront her, because she is ready for answers. Only the Lord can help us now. We hope we are doing the right thing."

It was morning and as Sharon went to the living room, to her surprise her grandparents were there waiting for her. She saw that breakfast had already been made. They dressed as if they were going somewhere. They both were looking at her with a serious look on their faces, not smiling. "Good morning Sharon," said her grandmother, "we were waiting for you, you slept a little late this morning." Sharon noticed something was quite different. Her grandparents were behaving strangely when they drank their tea. They were moving a bit cold. "I just overslept a little," answered Sharon.

"Nevertheless, you said you wanted answers, that is why we were waiting for you," Martha replied. "Come sit my dear and we will begin," said Alfred. "Please tell us when was the first time you started having these dreams and flashes as you called them." Sharon took a while before she could answer. "Concentrate my child we want to know how old you were when you started having these things."

Chapter *Three*

"I have seen it all my life, it is as if I have grown with these images," said Sharon. "If only we did listen to you, but we were trying to protect you the best way we could and after the incident we thought you couldn't remember anything." Sharon looked puzzled. "Couldn't remember what?" She asked. "Can you remember how old you were when you had your last dream? Think Sharon, think hard, it is very important for us to know how old you were," replied Martha. Sharon thought for a while and then answered. "Grandfather remember when you gave Ralphy a brand new pair of shoes for helping you do something?" asked Sharon.

"Yes I remember," answered Alfred. "Well, it was a little earlier than that when I started seeing these images that does not make sense." "So long ago," whispered Martha. There was silence.

"Well, are you going to answer my questions?" asked Sharon. "You see, after the last incident, you said you remembered wearing a red dress," said Martha. "Oh I love to dream about that, it makes me feel so safe and warm. I dreamt that I was responsible for safe keeping the compass. I remembered my father telling me to keep it in my pocket and not to let my sister and brother touched it. Then he would pat me on my head and said "off to work." I had a crown then," said Sharon.

As she spoke she closed her eyes tight so as to grasp every moment she could remember. When she opened her eyes she saw her grandparents sobbing. "Oh Sharon, Sharon it is time for you to know everything. Only God can help us now," said Martha.

Don't cry grandmother, please tell me what it is that I have to know, you are scaring me," said Sharon whose voice was shaking as she spoke.

"I am going to tell you something and I want you to listen very carefully," answered Martha. "The dreams and flashes you see are all real. They are images from your past. The initials in the compass is your father's initials," said Martha. "What, the initials in the compass is my fathers'?" asked Sharon. "Yes dear." "Tell me what was his name, I want to know," asked Sharon bursting with excitement.

"His name is King Daniel of Notting Hill," said Martha. Sharon was stunned. She thought she heard wrong. "What did you say?" Alfred held her hand. "Yes, you heard right. King Daniel of Notting Hill is your father which means you are a princess. The images are real darling. We thought things were just bundled up in your mind and we ignored them. Martha looked at her granddaughter so lovingly. She smiled and said "Sharon, my sweet Sharon, you are a true princess. That is why we are so protective of you.

Only after your eighteenth birthday you are supposed to know, but because of those images and the compass, we have no other choice." Sharon stood up and with a dazed look she repeated. "I am a princess?" She looked at her grandparents and asked. "I am a princess?" They both smiled and nodded positively and looked at each other holding each other hand with smiles in their faces.

Sharon began to pace up and down the room. "I am a princess?" she asked over and over. Then she stopped and began to laugh. "I am a princess. I am a princess. She then admitted to herself laughingly, "I am a princess." She kept on laughing and repeating, then hugged her grandparents with tears in both their eyes and smiling. Sharon suddenly became serious and asked herself. "I am a princess?" She was not laughing anymore, but spoke angrily, "I am a princess and you kept it from me all these years, all these years?"

The grandparents were silent. "You kept me here," and Sharon was silent. She had a puzzled look. "Grandfather you said father is king and his name is King Daniel of Notting hill, why did you say that?" He laughed and said, "that's because he is still alive, the king is still alive." Sharon became motionless, her eyes were opened wide and she was shocked, she could not speak for a while. "My father is alive?" she asked. "My mother and my brother and sister are all alive," she spoke to herself in a whispering voice. "I have a family," she said to herself. She was silent for a while, it was too much for her to take in at one time.

Then she turned around and asked with tears in her eyes. "Where are they and why am I not with them. Where are they grandmother and grandfather." "That is why we are protecting you so much, because something happened when you were a little girl. The last time we were all together you were wearing a red velvet dress and you had the compass for safe keeping," said Alfred."

"That was when your life changed drastically for you and everybody as well," answered Martha. Sharon was scared to ask what had happened. She was breathing heavily and the words could not come out all at once when she asked. "What happened?" They could not speak for a while, then her grandmother said, "We will tell you what we know so you will see clearly what happened. Can you recall anything else when you wore the red dress Sharon?"

Sharon thought for a while and said, "sometimes I saw myself running across the grounds somewhere with lots of shouting and noises in the background. I remember my brother and sister yelling for me to wait for them." "Where were you going dear?" asked grandmother. "I don't know, I heard my brother said I dropped my crown and I told him to run faster before the gate closed. "I ran so fast I had to wait on them at times, because the gate was already closing.

I heard my father said to keep running and don't turn around that I have to pass the gate before it closes, and I did passed it," said Sharon. "Yes you did dear, that's why you are with us today. Oh Sharon, you have grown to become such a beautiful princess. I am so proud of you for doing this," smiled Martha. Sharon was shaking and knelt beside her grandmother. She asked, "please tell me what happened, please?"

"You all lived very happily in the most beautiful castle you could ever imagine." She held on to Sharon hugging her tightly and continued. "I can just see it as if it was yesterday." Yes," said Alfred, "your father Daniel and your mother Elizabeth, Sharon they were deeply in love with each other.

The castle was filled with so much joy and laughter,

so many ball room dancing, parties and functions going on there. All the servants loved you so very much.

They loved your parents just as much. Daniel and Elizabeth never forgot the people who cared for them, who worked for them. They kept them close to their hearts. The maids, ministers and loyal subjects were all treated with respect. Sharon your father was a king to be envied by others and indeed he was envied."

"Elizabeth was his joy and you three were their pride and joy. Daniel was never too busy for his children." "Sharon, I remember very clearly the last ball room dance the castle had, your mother came down the stairs with your father beside her, held her hand gently, and kept looking at her every step he took. Your mother looked like an angel from heaven. She wore the most beautiful blue gown and looked the most beautiful too. That moment was so captivating. Her golden hair was let down in a most beautiful style. Oh what a magnificent sight it was indeed.

Daniel's face was glowing with happiness and pride when he introduced his queen to everyone. He always said that his wife was his shield and armor and she will reply as always, it is my love for you that is protecting you my darling." Martha continued to speak. "They danced as I watched them swirl across the room looking into each other's eyes. This wonderful moment lasted forever, until I was distracted when I heard Alfred shouting at Frank, your brother and Louisa your sister. They brought sparky (their dog) into the ball room and he was scampering all over the floor. Alfred was telling them to send him away before their clothes got soiled. That was when I saw you, my little princess.

It was a very auspicious day for the family indeed.

It was the day your father put your crown on your head. I remembered clearly. It had five gems each one representing a member of the family. You looked so beautiful wearing it. It was also your birthday my dear. You had the most beautiful red dress I ever saw. The servants could not take their eyes of you. You loved them also Sharon. They did everything for you. When you walked, you looked as if you were gliding across the room.

Your mother made the dress herself, she wanted you to look your best, since it was a very important day of your life," She continued," can you remember meeting anyone or dancing with anyone dear?" "No," answered Sharon. "Are you sure dear, think hard" said Alfred. "No, no one" replied Sharon. Martha turned to Alfred and said," you were with the children, did you see who she was dancing with Alfred?" "No, no I can't recall seeing her dancing at all," he said. "What happened next, grandmother?" asked Sharon. "You were supposed to meet a young prince that day.

I remembered him, he was so polite and charming. I remembered seeing him bowing to your parents with such grace. He was a sight to behold.

His parents said that they could not wait to see you dear." "Did I meet him?" asked Sharon. "I don't know, that was the last time I laid my eyes on him," replied Martha. "What about mother and father, what did they say about him?" asked Sharon. "I don't know, your mother told me once that King Paul and Queen Katherine were their very close friends. They have known each other a very long time and should something happen to either of the children, they put their trust on both parents.

"Sharon, it was a night to remember. I only saw the prince that night. I don't recall what happened next," said Martha. Alfred spoke, "my dear something did happened that night alright that changed the course of history a little. You see your father's invitation to the ball was far and wide. This ball was so very special to him all because or you. He did not forget anyone. I saw him checking over the list of invitees just not to forget anyone. Everyone came who got an invitation. There was one who came uninvited.

A woman and she changed the lives of everyone in the kingdom. Because of her, your parents are confined to their living quarters up till this day. Because of her, you came to live with us, because of her, you didn't remember your brother and sister.

She took the happiness, warmth and togetherness of the castle. The beauty of the kingdom is forgotten, only memories like what you have now dear," said Alfred very sadly. "Who was she grandfather?" asked Sharon. Alfred was lost for a while then smiled and said, "Her name is Rebecca, she knew your father all his life, before he met your mother. Rebecca and Daniel were a team once.

Daniel was always there for her and she did the same for him. Rebecca came from a very wealthy family who ran a mercantile operation in a number of countries around the world. Her parents were very proud people with one son to inherit the business one day. Rebecca and Daniel were very good friends. Daniel loved the outdoors, horseback riding, hunting, any kind of sports, you name it.

Chapter *Four*

Rebecca joined him lots of times. She also joined him for picnics, tea and dinners. Daniel had other girlfriends and boyfriends as well. They all would spend a lot of time just hanging out. Rebecca would asked Daniel sometimes if he was trying to make her jealous and she would reply that it was working. Daniel told her that she was being silly that he enjoyed all his friends and companions. Once when Rebecca heard that her face became serious. She did not like the answer she got.

As time passed Daniel became Rebecca's eyeball, she became obsessed with him which was unaware to Daniel. She prevented him from going horseback riding with anyone especially with the girls, only with her. She knew his every move until Daniel confronted her. "Well my darling what would you like to talk about? I hope it's not personal," she laughed. "No it's not Rebecca. I noticed lately that I don't spend time with anyone but you. I spoke to my friends and asked why they are avoiding me. They told me things that I never say to them, but you did, why Rebecca?" "Oh Daniel you worry for nothing she interrupted.

You and I know we are meant for each other. We are meant to be. That's why I don't think you should not waste your precious time to ordinary folks. You and I live in the same bracket, we don't need these people bothering us."

Daniel was puzzled. "These people, what are you talking about, they are my close friends and I love them all. What do you mean in the same bracket, I am the same as they." "Come on darling, we have the same status, my family and yours came from the same society so why not devote your time to me and no one else," replied Rebecca. "What, are you listening to yourself? Rebecca, these are my friends, my friends and I care for them a lot. I don't care about their background. They mean a lot to me," answered Daniel.

"But darling, she came closer to him and held his hand. "No, and he pushed her. Tell me what do you mean we are meant to be?" he asked. Rebecca then spoke. "You know my darling." "No I don't know, tell me," said Daniel. He was furious. "Well,she said "we are always in each other company, we share everything and one day we will get married and settle down my darling. You know one day you will rule the kingdom, that's why I'm preparing myself for you," she replied.

"Are you out of your mind? Who gave you the idea that I want to marry you." Rebecca was still smiling and said, "don't be silly dear." Daniel was very angry and answered. "Rebecca, I want you to listen to me carefully. I never once ask you for anything, because you never gave me the chance to ask, you are always there. You sent my friends away, tell them lies about me not being interested in them anymore because I have found you. Why Rebecca, why, I've always being a good friend to you."

"Darling, you are putting things out of proportion,"

she said smilingly. "Really Rebecca, you know we are just friends, just like the others, you are no different. Why are you doing this to us? I don't see you any different, and I never said that I will marry you, that is the furthest thing from my mind," said Daniel.

"You don't have to say it, but I know you want to," said Rebecca. "No, this is all in your mind, you wouldn't leave me alone, I'm just a friend," said Daniel. "Darling, just be rational about it "no," Daniel interrupted." you have gone too far, let's get everything straight, I want you to stop this right now." What do you mean my love," said Rebecca. "Don't call me love, I'm not your love," shouted Daniel angrily. "My sweetheart, how can I forget what we've been through together, you know there is no one else for you but me, and you know I'm always faithful," replied Rebecca. Daniel put his hand on his head and began to paste up and down. "I know you don't mean what you said, come on now you look tired and as she came closer to him, he said angrily, "Rebecca, get your hands off me."

With a deadly look in her face, Rebecca said, "That can't happen Daniel, you are very special to me. I don't know life without you. You are everything to me. You are mine, you have always been mine, don't deprive me of my happiness now. We are one, no one can separate us my love."

Daniel turned to her and looked deep inside her eyes and saw a very cold person for the first time. That, he had never seen before. He saw her for what she really was. He was not afraid of her, but became even more angry and said," I am saying this only once whether you like it or not. I will never marry you, you used me, try to take me away from everyone and lied to me.

We have nothing in common, I want you to leave and don't ever come to my castle again. I am very disappointed in you Rebecca you are a cold hearted selfish person who will tramp on anybody to get what you want. I am not your prize possession. We are all human beings and we are supposed to care and live for each other. That's what I did for you. I don't want to see you again until you change your attitude and ways of thinking.

Also you will apologise to everyone and speak the truth this time about us. Sometimes, I feel so drawn towards you, it's like I'm possessed or something. Thank God I'm back to my senses." Rebecca eyes became wide open. "Good bye Rebecca," said Daniel. He began to walk away when Rebecca held his hand.

"Tell me something before you leave Daniel, where have you been the last time we met?" "You would like to know, wouldn't you?" and shrugged himself away and left. Rebecca remained there speechless and motionless. "You felt as if you were possessed, ay Daniel, but not anymore? Why who is behind all this Daniel, who. You drifted away just like that, why?" She gave a heartless laugh, coming from her gut. "You stupid fool, do you think you can get away from me. I molded you to becoming mine. I waited and waited looking at you became a man, and now you left me just like that Daniel? Well, this is going to be interesting."

Daniel was devastated and remain alone for a while. He felt strange as if something evil came out of him. He said to himself, "thank God I got rid of her." After reflecting for a while, Daniel realized he never really knew who she really was. She was always in control. He decided to investigate the family and found out that the small businesses around could not compete with the family business at all. Some of the little owners told him that it was as if their hands were tied and her father and brother took everything from them. Daniel understood the feeling very clearly.

He investigated further and found out that Rebecca's family don't have friends. Their home was very close to the forest. People say they saw them go into the forest every full moon. They are scary people. When Daniel thought about what took place all he could conclude was that Rebecca's family dealt with black magic to get what they wanted and to be successful in life.

As time passed Daniel never give it any thought. Rebecca became a blur from his past. He had a wonderful life, full of success, happiness, hope and love, yes love. Remember when Rebecca asked Daniel who had drifted him away from her? Well here it is, the love of his life, Elizabeth your mother." "Mother" Sharon exclaimed. "Yes Sharon, your mother. She came into his life just in time to save him. She was his world and still is. I have never seen a blessed couple so happy and so full of life. Daniel never wanted anything else. Elizabeth gave him her undivided attention and loyalty. Life was long was peaceful, the citizens were happy with the running of the kingdom and when Daniel became king they were both married. The wedding was grand with playing of harps, trumpets, dancing and there was merriment everywhere. The roses in the rose garden looked even more beautiful and smelt even sweeter. Sharon Daniel was loved by all, and the world could not be more perfect. It was indeed heaven on earth," said Martha. "Then how did I end up living alone with you? Asked Sharon. Where is my family.

Where are they now?" "That my dear is where we all have to solve the puzzle, Martha, you and myself," answered Alfred. Sharon sat on the chair with despair. She was very scared to know what happened next. "That very night of the last ball room dance in the kingdom, everyone was just lost in enjoying themselves. The kingdom could not be more beautiful. The rose gardens were a sight to see. Even the sky with the stars and the moon that showed so brightly add lights to the wonderful colorful lights of the castle's surroundings.

Chapter *Five*

The setting was breath taking. The guests add beauty and grace as they came. There was joy and merriment everywhere. They loved their king so.

Then just like that, someone who was not invited suddenly showed up. She was dressed in black. She wore a long flowing gown. Her hair was let down and very black. She wore blood red lipstick. Indeed, she was a sight to look at. When she walked everyone gave a gasp when they saw her. She was pale in colour as if there was no blood in her, yet she looked astounding in a scary way. The guest moved aside for her to past. As she walked, she looked from side to side trying not to miss seeing anyone. Suddenly she stopped, abrupt when she saw the king and queen dancing.

She watched them looking at each other so lovingly. Her eyes were stuck on them for a long while. She was motionless and just kept staring at them. She came closer and closer until she caught their attention. The king and queen were taken by surprise, because she came right up to them. Rebecca looked at them, then at Daniel and with a very cold voice she spoke smilingly.

"Hello Daniel, miss me?" Daniel kept looking at her and to his surprise he could not believe his eyes.

Rebecca, is that you?" "I know you will not forget me, my love, after all these years. How long has it been, oh yes eleven years, you still remember, how sweet." By now everyone stopped dancing and the ball room became very quiet. She looked at Daniel straight in the eyes, looking at him without blinking as if she was drinking his beauty she had loved all her life. You could see that she was still madly in love with him. Her face was filled with sadness when she saw Elizabeth at the side of him.

This is the woman, she thought who has stolen her life and is living her dreams. As she thought of this her eyes became red with rage and she looked at Daniel. He just stared at her speechless. He then began to stutter as he asked "What are you doing here?" "Why Daniel, I came to the ball, everyone else is here." "Everyone is here with an invitation, you did not get invited." She began to laugh, "I don't need an invitation, we are one." "You are not invited here Rebecca, please leave." Rebecca became cold and serious and ignored him.

She started to move away and asked, "Can you bring me something to drink, my throat is a little dry." Daniel and Elizabeth looked at each other. "Rebecca, I want you to leave now or I will call the guards." Rebecca turned around looking at everyone and replied. "Why, what have I done my darling?"

"Look Rebecca," said Elizabeth, "don't you dare speak to me," said Rebecca in a very high pitch voice which caught the guests by surprise. They all gasped at once and became terrified of her, because her voice was harsh and evil. "You stole my husband from me," and with that she pushed her with such force, Elizabeth was sent flying towards the hall near the steps. The children screamed so did Elizabeth because it so sudden.

Daniel ran towards her. When he picked her up she was dizzy. It took a while before she was herself again. Rebecca began to laugh very loudly. Her laughter became louder and louder which sounded more like a witch cackling. While laughing, she span around, her gown began to lift to and fro. There were high wind and all of a sudden accompanied with lightning and thunder. People began to run and hide under tables and anywhere they can fit themselves. She stopped laughing at once and the room became quiet and peaceful once again.

Rebecca walked towards Daniel and with a low groaning voice she spoke." Daniel, you left me once but not this time." She pointed at him and pulled him with her magic. He tried very hard to prevent himself from gliding towards her. He tried to hold on to anything, but to no avail. "Come to me my love we belong together." "Not in this life." He made every effort to grab on to anything that can be a weapon to hit her. He got hold of a vase and flung it to her with all his might. Rebecca screamed and fell to the floor. Daniel ran towards his queen, but Rebecca was waiting for them. Her eyes were red in color and she gave a shrieking laugh that could pierced the daylight out of anyone. She spoke with a groaning voice and said, "it's time that I finished you two once and for all."

As she was about to raise her hand, Elizabeth spoke. "Wait, stop, let's talk about this calmly and quietly." "Wait you said? I have been waiting for eleven years since you told me to leave Daniel. "I never meant any harm Rebecca, I just told you to leave, so that you can reflect on your bad actions. I didn't know you took it so seriously." "You moron, you imbecile, I must leave just because you said so. Forget what we have shared all our lives because you said so. Forget that we ever existed, right Daniel? You pretended you care and then toss me away, all because of this idiot you call your wife?" "That was a long time ago," answered Elizabeth, "what do you want from him?"

"What do I want from him? I'm glad you asked, since this does not concern you. He has done enough, it's what I'm going to do now. I have waited so long for this moment. "Daniel, you left me broken hearted, couldn't care if I die or not, you discarded me, threw me out of your kingdom. You had no feelings for me all along. You took me for a ride." Her eyes were wide open as she recalled her past with Daniel. "You took me for granted, while I was always there for fulfilling your every needs and this is what I got in return." "Rebecca," said Elizabeth, Daniel told me about you, you never told him how you felt, he didn't know, please don't blame him, he's innocent, he saw you as a very dear friend, someone who he could confide in."

"Silence you imbecile, interrupted Rebecca. "How dare you address me, it's you, you are the one who stole him from me. I had him on my grip until you came along. What kind of power do you have that is greater than anything that I came across? Just like that, he disappeared." "Love, Rebecca, it's called love. I fell in love with my wife, a very warm, understanding, caring, kindhearted, I can go on and on, unlike you Rebecca, he was looking at Elizabeth as he spoke.

"Oh Daniel, this is too much," she said laughingly. Elizabeth turned to her and said "I will not allow to say another word again. I want you to leave this instant, you have disturb us enough, now you must leave." She pointed the entrance of the kingdom and with a stern look she ordered Rebecca to leave. "This is the second time I have been thrown out of this kingdom." She began to laugh and laugh turning around at the same time. "Oh, this is too much you know, I'm being thrown out again, but not this time Elizabeth, not this time." "What ever do you mean Rebecca?" asked Daniel.

"My dear queen, just as Daniel deprived me of my love, so too you will be deprived of yours." She made a groaning sound as she raised her hands. A strong wind began to blow throughout the entire building accompanied with lightning and thunder. The chandeliers were swaying to and fro. Everything was blown all over the kingdom. The wind was so powerful that the tables and chairs were sent flying across the hall. There was dust everwhere, it was difficult to see anything. The noise was too harsh and the sound coming out of Rebeccas' mouth was horrifying. She looked like the goddess of death. Her eyes were blood red and were opened wide as she swirl herself around until the wind lifted her into the air.

Her hair was all over and looked like it became alive as she spoke with a horrifying voice. "Just as I was left all alone in the dark with no one, so shall you become, Elizabeth, you will have no love, no one to love. You will feel cold inside you even though there will be warmth around you. Your husband will be no more, there shall be darkness all around you and whatever and whoever you touched will wither away. This is my curse to you. I have waited eleven years for this moment and so shall it be for I shall reside in this kingdom with you so there shall be no escape.

Chapter *Six*

"Stop this nonsense at once," ordered Daniel but to no avail. "My sweet Daniel, just as you have abandon me from your life, so too you will be abandon from your queen. All you can do is to watch her shadow as she pass by for the very glimpse of her eyes that fall on anyone they will die instantly.

You all will wither and become dust. You will suffocate and die. It is your turn to suffer." Elizabeth fell unconscious. I have something specially planned for your children." "No, no not my children, I beg you to leave them alone, they are innocent." "You all will pay," she said. Daniel ran for his sword, but was too late. Rebecca twirl her hand and send him across the hall. He called out for his children. "Here we are father, help us." They were hidden under the steps scared to even breathe. Daniel ran for the sword once more and as Rebecca was about to grab the children, he swung the sword at her. "Don't you dare touch them," he yelled.

The sword hit her in her stomach, she screamed with pain and fell to the floor. Daniel took hold of his family and began to run away from her. The guest did the same. There was helter skelter everywhere with a lot of shouting and screaming. Daniel ran through the flower garden and kept on saying, "run children, run, do not be afraid I am with you." Before he could get far Rebecca came in front of them. "Rebecca, leave my kids alone. He fought with her, but he was no match for her. She tossed him on the grass. He rolled over and over while saying "run children, don't let her catch you." "Not one of your family can leave you fool, this is my curse.

Elizabeth was thrown back inside the kingdom. Daniel threw the compass towards Sharon and told her to not to lose it. He shouted to Sharon and told her to keep running as fast as she could before the castle gate closed. Sharon did as she was told, her brother and sister could not catch up with her. Sharon heard them say to slow down they can't meet her but she listened to her father and kept running. She came out of the gate before it closed leaving her loved ones inside with Rebecca. She was out of breath and was very tired from running so fast.

She was not so sure where she was, all she knew was that she was outside the castle and away from the gate.

When Rebecca saw that she was out of the gate, she began to laugh once again. "You can go my dear, you are not needed here. I've gotten something from you that is more precious than you yourself." She then turned to Daniel and said, "do you know what it is oh king, her hair. Look it is implanted on my head," She turned and showed Daniel.

What he saw was a shriek of golden hair which glowed in her head. It shone so bright he was dazzled. "This hair will tell me where you all are and I will know every move you make in the kingdom. Sharon heart is the purest of all she will guide me and I will know what you are up to. If on her eighteenth birthday she does not save you, your entire kingdom will be perished. Your sweet children and wife will no longer exist. That will be my satisfaction.

You threw me out of here, now everything exists here is mine all mine and everyone in it. Now you will know the mistake you've made by excluding me from your life. I'm supposed to be Queen of Nothing Hill. Now the time has come for me to take what is mine." She began to laugh and rose up in the air. The wind started to blow angrily in all directions, with such rage that the tables and chairs flew up and down. There was a sudden uproar. The villagers heard the noise and became alert. They held each other as the noise became louder and louder. The animals began to run up and down sensing some kind of danger while making noises as well.

The trees swayed to and fro. The roses in the gardens were hurled unto the air with petals of all colors flying everywhere. The most frightening of all was the noise that was emanating from this. It was so excruciating, Daniel and the children stayed on the ground holding their ears. They could not move because the wind was gushing from all directions. Beyond all that noise Rebecca's laughter could be heard loud and clear. She remain in the air and looked at the entire castle as she continued to laugh in a horrific voice.

As she came down and touched ground everything began to subside. It became silent again. She spoke as she saw Daniel. "This kingdom will now become barren with no lights no merriment or laughter. There will be no happiness, no music of any kind. It will be lifeless, with no colors or taste. Nothing will grow but twigs and thorns. As she spoke the sky became very dark and the kingdom began to change exactly as she predicted.

The fountain lights were out and the water stopped flowing. The roses became frailled and withered. There was a deadly silence. Rebecca turned to Daniel and said, "I will not leave here not until Sharon came to fulfill her needs. This kingdom is mine, I am in charge here. I will reside where no one can see me, but where I can see all." The castle was changed into a dungeon. The forest surrounding the castle became thicker.

The vines were huge and began to wrap around the entrances and windows of the castle. The changes she made outside the castle looked dark and gloomy. Anyone who came near would shiver with fright. The main gate looked like twigs and vines that covered the gate totally. There was thunder and lightning everywhere.

Daniel shouted to the children to get back inside the kingdom for safety. They were so scared and cried for their mother. They called out to her. When they found Elizabeth, they shook her until she was awaken. "A wicked lady is trying to kill us all," cried Michael. When she came to her senses Rebecca was right in front of her. "Hello my queen, we meet again. Elizabeth was startled. She made a swing at Rebecca, but hit her head instead and fell once more on the floor. This did not stop her, "leave my children alone, do not touch them, you hear me you witch. Run for cover my children, I'll deal with her once and for all." Rebecca flew in the air and landed in front of her again. Elizabeth could not reach the sword in time. "No sword can kill me." Elizabeth tried to get up but fell again. "You don't give up easily do you?' Elizabeth got up and ran for the sword and said, "never, I will fight for my family because they are my life. All they know is love not hate.

I told you once to leave us alone but never again. She swung the sword but Rebecca had already vanished, she was behind her. "How touching you love your family so much, now it is time for the curse to take effect on you. Rebecca raised her hands and pointed them to Elizabeth and said. "You will only be a shadow in the wall when your loved ones call, when they need you, you will but fall for you will become as cold as snow and because of the curse they are yet to know." With that she spread her hands to strike Elizabeth, but the sword was still in Elizabeth's hand and caught Rebecca's reflection which went right back at her.

With a loud scream she disappeared. All Elizabeth could hear was a cold shivering mourning sound which faded somewhere in the castle. When she followed the sound that vanished she saw a shadow on the wall of the kingdom. It was Rebecca's. The curse had already began to take effect on Elizabeth. Some of her hair were on the floor, and she looked very pale and weak. Daniel came running towards her. She remembered the curse and cautioned Daniel not to look at her and to keep the children away from her. She spoke in a very weak voice and collapsed.

Daniel was very saddened indeed, he knew he could not help her. The curse was very strong and he was helpless. He was very saddened to see what became of his life and family. "Daniel my love remember the curse, you are not to look at me or touch me just hear my voice and we will communicate this way. This goes to the children as well. Be strong and with prayers and the love we have for each other, we will overcome this some day. Farewell for now my sweet king." Daniel slumped to the floor motionless with no life in his body. Rebecca was no where to be found.

The queen was a very strong and powerful person. She would do anything for her family. She left her family and went in one the rooms and stayed there so that no one will die if they see her. She sank herself in the bed and sighed. "My only hope is with my daughter. I will remain here until she becomes eighteen years. I shall continue to fight this curse for the protection of my family.

As Sharon hair grows so will her mind becomes stronger and stronger. Her heart is pure and because of this she will be able to bring back the family together and the curse will be lifted. My sweet innocent child, my prayers will always be with you. You will never be alone for our love for you will bind us together. Her hair will be the key for her success and as it glows so will her powers."

Suddenly Elizabeth heard Rebecca's footstep getting closer and closer towards her then stop, then started again. Elizabeth stood still. Rebecca was on the other room and looked at the mirror. She was surprised to see herself and asked, "how could this be, I'm supposed to be cursed, but what happened and where's Sharon's hair where is the gold strand?" Elizabeth was surprised when she heard Sharon's name and was puzzled.

Rebecca was also shocked. "Well well, what luck this is. Sharon's hair lifted the spell off me and gave me another chance. Oh Daniel, if you only know, now I have another chance with you, thanks to your very own daughter." Elizabeth was furious and at the same time saddened. "Oh no no, no one must know of this, I must find that girl. She is my life support," she spoke heartily.

When Elizabeth heard that, she was about to spring on her when Daniel stroke Rebecca with his sword. "Let's see who is going to save you this time." Rebecca laughed, "you foolish man, no one can kill me except your very own daughter, and she is not here now, is she Daniel, it is just you and I." Before she could complete her sentence Daniel rush out of the room to save himself.

The sword fell off his hands as he ran. Rebecca began to cast another spell on Daniel when Elizabeth ran in front of him with the sword she caught. Once again the spell was reflected on her and she screamed. This time she had no hair to save her, it can only save her once and she will remain a shadow until the spell was broken. Elizabeth could not grasped what the spell was but heard laughter on the wall and realized she was cursed. She moved away from him. "Don't go," he said. "I have to my darling because of the curse. Take care of our children, don't ever let them come close to me. With this she became very old and began to bend and walk.

She went into a room, locked herself in and wept for a long while. She wept for a while longer, then got up and looked into the mirror. What she saw was an old woman, pale and thin with no expression on her face.

Her eyes were sunk in and her golden hair became grey. She had lost her beauty. "Why? She asked herself, what have I done to deserve this." She felt lonely and cold and knew the curse was upon her. Daniel explained everything to his children. The castle was closed with just a few servants remaining. Everything that was alive was gone. The children felt cold and Daniel hugged them.

As the sun rose, streaks of light came bursting into the castle. The servants tried to open the windows and doors but could not. Inside the castle there was hardly any light at all, especially where Rebecca resided. Elizabeth awoke and opened the window in her room. The sun was warm and loving yet she was cold and moved away from the sun. Even though she loved the sun, it irritated her because of the curse. Daniel and the children could only use part of the castle. The servants took care of them. They were well taken care of. After breakfast Daniel tried to find Elizabeth, but could not reach far for Rebecca's reflection was watching and she was laughing. The servants had no effect from the curse, they did what they had to do for Elizabeth and then left. They were all very afraid of Rebecca.

One day, Elizabeth began to sing a beautiful song. The children heard her and began to call her. She realized that she can communicate with them through her voice. They ran passed the corridor and reached her room "Mummy, open the door, we want to see you." "No my darlings, I can talk and sing to you, but I can't let you in." Rebecca became uneasy and began to create havoc by throwing things all over the place.

Chapter *Seven*

Elizabeth answered and said, "don't be scared, she can't hurt you, our love for each other is the only weapon we have to fight her. Don't be afraid, but stay away from her for she will try to harm you." They lived like that waiting for Sharon to return. Only at night Elizabeth will look outside and watched the moon and stars for the daylight is too strong for her eyes. Whenever it was raining then she would look outside.

Sharon's grandparents would visit them whenever the servants send an invitation. The compass was used for them to know which direction they could meet Daniel and the children. They were to follow specific instructions. Rebecca can move from wall to wall but confined herself to stay close to Elizabeth's room. They would normally meet outside the castle where there were no walls. The meetings were very brief. Elizabeth would informed them through her songs about Rebecca's whereabout. Sometimes she would look outside and watched them when the weather was right for her.

As time passed by Daniel also became very pale and thin, just living for his family and waiting. There was sadness in the entire castle. The servants did a wonderful job by planting crops, maintaining the gardens and taking care of grounds. Daniel complimented them on a number of occasions. He even worked with them many times with his children. It was very sad indeed for the servants to see their king in that condition.

They even told him it was a pleasure indeed to be with him and not home. They were very happy to serve him and to share his sadness with him.

The grandparents brought whatever they need. Rebecca was always looking at them from inside. At times she would be very loud with her scream and mourning just to be heard and to scare the daylights out of them. At nights Elizabeth will sing to her family which will comfort them and put them to sleep. The servants would smile when they heard her singing. That was the only comfort in the castle, listening to the queen's voice.

"Sharon, this is why your birthday is so important. Can you remember anything else dear?" She looked at her grandmother and said. "I remembered everything else. Before Rebecca made her entrance, my father introduced me to Prince Phillip. Yes that is his name. We talked for a while. We shared a brief moment together. I showed him the compass and he said he liked it. He said he was happy to be at the ball and to have met me. I was ten, and he was twelve.

He behaved mature for his age. Where ever I went he followed. He said he liked me and gave me this ring. It was his mothers'. He said that I'm his princess and I just laughed. He said goodbye to me at the rose garden and that I was the star of that eventful night. Where is he prince now?" she asked. "No one has heard of him or has seen him since," replied Martha. "All I remembered is that someone grabbed me from behind. It was too noisy and dark. I felt a cold hand and I tried to get away.

He grabbed me and held my mouth. I fought him and then we heard noises coming towards us he threw me on the ground and I hit my head. I don't know what happened next." "You lost your memory then, my dear," said grandma. "How am I going to lift this curse?" "From your heart," Martha smiled. Your heart is as pure as gold, so precious and divine." Sharon slumped on the chair and thought of her prince. "Where are you my prince?"

The villagers would normally hunt in the forest together once in a while with their bow and arrows and other weapons. Sharon decided to be a part of the team that year. They would hunt just for fun. They were all excited. Everyone boasted what they would bring back. Sharon was very skillful at bow and arrows and handling swords, but does not kill animals. Her grandfather taught her well. While they were in the forest, they were separated.

Sharon decided to do some sight seeing since it was new to her. She didn't realized that the group were ahead of her and took another route. She kept looking at the tall trees which were huge. Suddenly, she heard voices approaching and saw three men walking and talking and pointing directions. They did not look like any of the villagers she knew. She then realized that she was alone without the group. Sharon noticed that one was well built and handsome. The other two were taking orders from him. "Harry, Smithy, come here," she heard him say. "What is it my lord?" "Look, a mother and her young ones, go try and save them before the others come." Sharon listened to their conversation and followed them.

At one time she lost them and when she turned, she saw them. "Well, well, well, what have we here, are you lost?" said one. "O no, I'm familiar with the forest." "Really, then why are you alone, and not with others." "I was following a deer and ended up here." "Oh I see, then where's the deer, I don't see anything." "You must have scared him away. "I'm sorry we all will help you look for it," answered the guy. "Thank you," said Sharon. They looked for a while and found nothing. "Well he must be very far away now," the guy said.

"I'm so sorry for taking up your time," said Sharon. "Madam, the pleasure is all mine," and he bowed at her. Sharon began to head back to the others but realized she was lost. The gentleman noticed that and looked at his two friends with a smile. "Are you looking for something else my lady?" he asked. "No, I'm just tired, I need to rest a while," she said. "Do you mind if we join you?" "No not at all as a matter of fact, I'm glad that you are here." "Why is that?' he asked. He was teasing her.

She noticed that because he knew she could not find her way to her friends. He looked at her closely and admired her long golden hair. "Your hair is very beautiful I must say," said the gentleman. "You reminded me of someone I knew a long long time ago." "Thank you," giving him the crossed eye. She also gave a complete look at him and thought to herself. "You are not bad yourself." Even the hair and bushy beard looked good on him. "Bye the way, my name is George, and this is Harry and Smith." The two men bow at her without speaking. "Harry, did you hear something?" "Yes, voices coming from the opposite direction."

"Those are my friends, I must be going now, good bye," said Sharon. "Wait," he said and held her arm. She looked at him. "We will accompany you until you reached them. She agreed.

"Where do you live?" "Just outside the forest, near the oak tree, can't miss it, and you?" she asked. "I am not from here." "I gather that much," said Sharon. "I'm a woodcutter and a swordsman. I know the forest very well."

"Okay, here we are thank you once again." "Wait, if you need anything from the forest, I can help you with that." Harry and Smithy both shook their heads positively. "I don't go out often, my grandfather is very protective of me," she said. "We have some work here, so we'll be around, good bye." She looked and noticed he was looking at her strangely. "I'm sorry, it's just that you reminded me of someone I once knew. "Smithy turned to Harry and said "he needs to get out this jungle." They both laughed. "Seriously guys, it is true, especially her hair, I've seen hair like that before." Harry and Smithy were trying very hard not to burst out laughing but could not. "Oh, what beautiful hair you have Harry." "Thank you Smithy, you know I took a lot of time grooming," he said in a feminine manner.

They both shout out laughing. George walked away in a daze thinking of Sharon. "I know I have seen that before. It was too real to ignore. Harry and Smith saw that George was very quiet and was in deep thought with himself. "Hey, what's with him?" They came to him and Smithy asked, "are you all right my lord?" "Not so loud," said George. "Don't worry we're are safe, we didn't mean to make fun of you," said Harry. "Listen boys, seeing her the memories of the princess came to me as I saw her golden hair."

"We are so sorry, my lord we didn't know, please forgive us." George sat there for a while and then decided to head back. Harry and Smithy became sad as they watched George walking. "How long again Harry, how long again can he live in disguise." "Your guess is as good as mine, he is just trying to be brave but we know he is missing his life."

Chapter *Eight*

"Come along boys," and they hurried towards him. Sharon was very happy to have met George. She didn't tell anyone about him. George was very curious about Sharon. As he laid on his cot under the stars and the moon shining down on him he recollected his meeting with her. "Who is she, why do I feel that I've met her before?" he said out loud. "She reminded me of someone, but who." He tried hard to remember, but to no avail. Sharon on the other hand, was combing her hair and was lost while looking at the moon. "I would like to see him again," she said to herself. His touch was so soft yet he looked rugged.

Next day Sharon was very anxious to go to the edge of the forest. "Bye grandmother, I'm going to see the rabbits, be back soon." The rabbits would come out early in the morning with their kids to feed before being disturbed by the villagers. Sharon laughed with glee when she saw them. Her hair was down and the wind was blowing in her face.

She ran and skipped as she approached them. "How cute you are, you are a sight to see, you know that." "I think so too," said George trying to look his best. "Good morning," she said shyly. "It is indeed a beautiful one," butt in Harry. Smithy could not believe his eyes when he saw Harry cleaning himself and smiling with Sharon. He grabbed him at the back of his neck and said, "we have so much work to do today, let's go.

You fool can't you see George is interested in her. What do you think you were doing there?" "I didn't see him, I thought she was talking to me," replied Harry. "That's because you are more than a fool, you know that." "Hello, we meet again," said George. "Yes," answered Sharon. "What are you doing here so early?" he asked. "I came to see the rabbits, aren't they wonderful, touching one of them. "Yes," he said looking at her hair as she stood against the sun. The forest looked so romantic to both of them. The birds were singing. The sunlight came peeping through the tall trees. The wind blew gently and there was a symphony of sound everywhere. it was indeed a beautiful sight to behold.

The stream made such rippling sound as the animals came to quench their thirst. Sharon and George enjoyed the sight and with smiling faces they looked at each other. Sharon asked the same question. "What are you doing here so early." "Well I live in the forest I have a tree house, not too far from here." "You mean you actually live in the forest, on a tree house? she asked. I always wanted a tree house but my grandfather wouldn't allow it, says it's too dangerous. Can I see it please?' Smilingly, he said, "yes of course you can. "Let's not waste any time let's go." You could see the excitement on her eyes. "Uh, you mean right now? The workers are not here yet." Sharon saw that he was hesitating to go which confused her. "Don't you want me to see your tree house?' she asked. "Uh, today is not good, perhaps another time." Smithy and Harry were not far away when they heard their conversation and decided to help him. Harry turned to Smithy and said, "oh come on slow poke, we have a lot of work to do."

"Oh hi again we came to ask George if the water we are carrying will be enough since we have a long way to go." "I'm sure there will be rivers and streams on the way back," said George. They nodded and left. "I'm sorry for thinking of myself alone," said Sharon. "There is no need to apologize," he answered. Sharon looked at him as he spoke and she liked what she saw. George knew she was checking him out and was impressed. "Well, see you tomorrow then." Yes, yes of course I'll be right here, good bye," she said.

Sharon never felt so about anyone before. She had a smile on her face when she came home. She was in a happy mood indeed and sang while doing her chores. Her grandparents saw the change in her. "She looks just like her mother, don't you think so dear. I hope the mood she is in does not go away," said Martha. George and his servants began to clean the tree house, and its' surroundings. He hid the important stuff away so that Sharon would not know his true identity. Harry and Smithy, his loyal subjects made sure of that.

"You can have your bath now, your highness," said Harry. "Who are you calling your highness, what if someone hears us you fool." Replied Smithy. "Well there is no one here for more than a mile or so, no one can hear us," said Harry. "You are so naïve, don't you know even the trees can hear us. We don't know what that co called King is up to, so please, please be very quiet," exclaimed Smithy. "Is that so?" "Yeah that's so," and the two began to argue with each other. "There are so many things put in the ground so that when someone steps on them we will hear them, as if you don't know Smithy." "Well you can't be too careful." They continued to argue.

"Come on you guys, cut that out will you? George said in a soft voice. You two have done enough, I don't know how I could have survived without you. You are more than my servants, you are my support. You do everything for me you even think for me as well. You both mean a lot to me, I thank you very much." He gave them a hug. "Aw, it's nothing, we are here to serve you, your highness, we should thank you for getting this opportunity to serve you your highness," said Smithy."

"I wonder what Sharon would say when she found out that I'm not the person whom she thought I am." "Well, enjoy the moment while you can, 'cause this one is a winner ent it Smithy," said Harry. "She sure is." George was in deep thought and said to himself. "I'm so very far from home, when will it all end?"

"Your highness, do you know her from the past?" asked Harry, who was the more intelligent of the two. "That's what puzzled me so, she reminded me of someone. I can't remember anything else, said George. As you all know, I never had a social life as long as I can remember. My kingdom has been taken away from me, I'm on the run and the castle is being held by you know who." "They all thought you are dead by now, no one has seen us since," said Harry "Let's hope for the best, the important thing is that we are alive," said George. "Your highness, since you never had a social life for so long, then Sharon reminded you of someone in the past, when you were very young," said Harry. "Could be," said George.

Sharon prepared herself for the next day. She made brownies and carried water and cherries. When she arrived, George was waiting for her. He saw the excitement in her eyes, he was also excited. The journey was a bit far. Sharon didn't mind at all. They talked and talked, rested on the river banks, stopped to look at the animals. They laughed and ate. Then they came to a dense thick forest. "Where do you go from here?" she asked. "Follow me," said George. He led the way and Harry and Smith cleared the way for them.

Sharon noticed it was a hidden path. George told her to be careful where she put her feet while she walked. He told her to follow his footsteps. She did as she was told. "Here we are," he said finally. When she looked up she was so taken back. She was not expecting to see a tree house like that. "Oh it's so beautiful, I've never seen anything so beautiful before. Did you build this?' "Yes, and with the help of my two helpers here."

Sharon stood gazing at the tree house. It was built on one of the largest trees in the forest that had its' branches and trunk spreading out wide. It was so well built. She looked at the craftsmanship of it. It was not just a tree house, but an art. To begin to describe it, it was huge, with porches, windows and swings. The steps were so well crafted. Sharon could not take her eyes of it. The furnitures were amazing in every room and porch. "This house is fit for a king," she said. The surroundings were well groomed with a flower garden and swings.

The roses were of multiple colors. It was a rainbow of colors. She was so happy she came and she turned around and around running and jumping and laughing so heartily. "Oh George this place is fit for a king," as she span around. The wind blew her hair up and touched George. "I keep myself busy with Harry and Smith here. When she came back to them out of breadth of course, she gave George the brownies she made which he shared with the other two. Sharon saw a swing between two large trees and ran towards it like a little girl. It was decorated with beautiful flowers. George followed her. As she swung the wind blew her hair.

Chapter *Nine*

She closed her eyes and said, "this is a dream, a perfect dream, everything is perfect." She looked at the tree house and realized that how it was built, it was blended with the color of the leaves and other trees around so that it would not be noticeable. Someone has to take a good look at It to realise that it is a house on a tree. "Am I perfect for you?" asked George as he watched her swing. She stopped swinging and said, "I have never had so much fun. I never knew life could be so beautiful, until now." "You have a very good insight, you know how to transform this place into a haven," she said laughingly and began to swing again. George pushed the swing higher.

They both talked and laughed and enjoyed each others' company. "How I wished this day will never end." "So do I, answered George. You didn't answer my question," he reminded her. "Am I perfect for you? "She stopped the swing and apologize for not answering. "I'm sorry George, I have to leave now." "What, you just got here." "I know, but this is wrong." "What are you talking about, you just said that everything was perfect." "I really have to go." She began to leave. "Wait, where are you going, why are you leaving so suddenly.?"

"I'm sorry, I should have never led you on." "Well, it's too late." He held her hand. "Don't go, whatever it is, we can fix this." "No you don't understand, I have to go." "You are not going anywhere until you tell me what is wrong,"

George insisted. "It has nothing to do with you, it's something I have to do alone," she answered. "I'm not letting you go until you tell me what is going on..."

"George, please understand, I really have to go." "Something tells me that I wouldn't see you again if you leave, that's why I'm not letting you go. You are afraid of something or someone, tell me, we will fix this." he said firmly. Sharon covered her face and began to cry.

"How could I do this, I forgot all about my family. My parents are depending on me, how could I forget." "Sharon, I'm here for you, just let me help you, I'm not going to lose you," said George. He removed her hands from her face and they looked at each other. "O George," and she hugged him.

They held each other for a while and she spoke. "You understand me so well." She began to cry again. "Don't cry," and wiped her tears away. "I'm not supposed to feel this way about anyone besides my prince," she said. George became alert when he heard prince. "What prince?" There was silence for a while.

"Sharon I care a lot about you. I think I'm in love with you." "I feel the same way about you too George but this should not be happening." "What do you mean you can't feel this way about anyone besides the prince. I don't understand, please tell me." Sharon looked at him and felt sorry for what she had done. "I'm supposed to be in love with a prince who can help me break the curse from a wicked woman. What is going to happen now," she said. "Where does the prince live?" asked George. "I don't know."

They both remained silent and then George spoke, "tell me what happened from the beginning." "I can't remember clearly, but I was only ten when my life turned upside down." "Ten you say." "Yes. That's one thing I am sure of, because it was my birthday." "Your birthday, you say."

It reminded me when I was young, I had a friend who celebrated her tenth birthday also. Tell me what happened." "Everything and everyone had left. I lost everyone except my grandparents. It's like a blur, I don't know where to begin." "You said you were ten right, that's a start. Say anything you remember that's a start, it does not have to make sense.

Just keep on talking and everything will fall into place." "Well I know It was my birthday and there was a ball at the castle." "Castle, did you say castle?" "Yes, and there was a ball there." "You mean you got invited to the ball in the castle?" "No silly, it was the ball that was in honor of my birthday." George looked confused, so did Harry and Smithy who crept up and listened to every word they were saying. "Keep talking," said George. You wouldn't believe that I was a princess once. I still am but because of the curse I'm not but I will be once again," said Sharon. "O.K," he said as he tried to understand what she had just said. "Go on." "Everything was going so well at the ball. There were dancing, music and lot of food and drinks.

Everyone were just enjoying themselves, there was merriment everywhere. I've have never experienced anything like that again in my life." "Why?" "That's when she came in unannounced, like a black demoness, devouring everything in her path." Sharon told George everything as if it was yesterday. As she spoke there was sadness in her face. Sometimes George had to console her when emotions ran high.

Also Harry and Smith showed their emotions as well. When she spoke of Rebecca they became so afraid of her and was shaking. "Sharon, did you meet anyone at the ball that night?" asked George. "No, she said, there was chaos everywhere, that witch left no stone unturned, she made sure of that." George thought for a while. "This Rebecca, did she had a brother?" he asked. "Why, yes, how do you know?' "Is his name Edward?" "That I know for sure. How do you know his name, they are so evil both of them. Did you had an encounter with him, somewhere in the forest?" she said.

"You said you were ten and are you sure you did not meet anyone that night? Think hard and try to remember. "Yes George, you are right, I do remember. I met Prince Phillip that said night. Ever since we met, he is always on my mind. He is the one I live for, until I met you. I think my love has been transferred from him to you. I don't know what to do now." "I know what you can do. Sharon did the prince give you a ring?" Harry and Smith could hardly breathe when they heard the name Prince Phillip. They continued to listened quietly. "Yes he did, I always keep it close to my heart in a chain," and she pointed her heart.

"My eighteenth birthday is around the corner and time is running out." "Does the ring has two arrows touching with sparks in it?" asked George. "How do you know, yes of course it does," said Sharon confused and puzzled. "Oh my God, I hope I didn't drop it," "No no you didn't," George said before she could continue. He held her hands and George recalled what Prince Phillip told her that night."This is a symbol of my love, it will keep on growing as long as it is you." Sharon completed the sentence. "You have taken my heart and now it is with you."

George came closer to her and slowly removed the beard and other disguise. To her surprise a very handsome prince was in front of her. "I'm your Prince Phillip, Sharon. She was speechless. Harry and Smith were so taken up with the conversation, they didn't realized they were moving backwards and to and fro that they almost fell of a cliff.

They held each other tightly and sighed. "Prince Phillip, this can't be how are you my Prince Phillip?" George looked at her so lovingly and replied. "Yes my love we have found each other. You see, before Rebecca made her appearance, I left with my parents. I was pushed inside the chariot and my dad told the driver to make haste but to no avail. There was a man in black robe who rode next to the chariot beckoning him to stop. When he did he jumped inside the chariot and put a dagger on my father's neck.

I remembered my mother begged him not to kill him or any of us. The man had on a mask and he was so furious. He hit my mom in her head with his other hand and she fell unconscious. I cried out "mother". My father begged him to stop what he was doing. He said he would give him anything just to let us go. The man was breathing very heavily and began to yell at him. He said that was the answer to everything money, position and status and his sister had none of it. The bandit told my dad that things are going to change.

He said Queen Elizabeth, your mother had taken Daniel from his sister. Now he would take me away from them. He watched my father and said "That's fair enough, don't you think." After that incident, all I could remember was that I was in room by myself when a maid came in and opened the door.

She said," breakfast time, eat up now for the new king has plans for you," and she laughed.

"New king, what new king," said Phillip. "Don't play games with me, lad, you know fully well what I mean. Since your parents passed away King Edward took over. Thank God your father had a distant brother to rule this kingdom," the maid answered. "What are you talking about?" asked Prince Phillip. "My mother and father," he was interrupted by the maid. "Yes yes, they are no more, it has been almost a week now. You were badly bruised when king Edward found you. Thank God your father had asked to meet him, when he saw the creature of a man trying to rob you all in the carriage. He heard your father yelled for help and king Edward, your uncle came to his rescue. Thank God for him," said the maid.

The young prince listened attentively and knew that everything was a lie. While the maid was talking he recalled what actually took place that night. He waited for the maid to say something more. Well eat up then, and go straight downstairs for your new king wants to talk to you." Prince could hardly walk down the stairs.

Every step he took was like a lifetime. He didn't know what to think, what to say and most frightfully who is uncle Edward. Before he could reached the bottom of the stairs, he was startled by a heavy voice, unlike his fathers' saying, "I don't have all day, hurry up and come here. Didn't you eat breakfast?" When Phillip raised his head, he saw the same man who attacked his parents on their way home to the castle.

He stood there and just stared at the man in front of him. They looked at each other with Edward studying him as he paced in front of him. Phillip was disgusted at the look of Edward and also looked at him closely and wanted to puke. Phillip could not adjust to living without his parents and to have a new uncle he never knew existed. He knew he had to listen to his every words for now. He needed more information from hearing what people were saying and tried to figure what was happening.

He knew that Edward would make his life a living hell because he knew the truth. Edward then spoke. "Come here boy, beckoning him." He looked like a monster in Phillip's eyes. As Phillip walked closer towards him he grabbed him with such unexpected force which caused Phillip to scream out. He was so close to Edwards' face. Phillip looked at him with large open eyes full of fright. Edward said, I know you remembered what happened that night. Let me make myself very clear.

Chapter *Ten*

If you ever reveal the truth to anyone and I mean anyone, you will be beheaded, instantly. Do you hear me, and before I do that, I will torture you in such a way, you will beg me to kill you. Is that clear?" Phillip nodded his head. "I am your uncle now, and whatever I say you will listen without thinking. Do I make myself clear?" Phillip nodded his head again. "I'm sorry, I didn't quite get that." "Ye, yes," said Phillip whose voice was choked. "Good, you are not to say anything, I'll do the explaining to everyone. All you have to do is pretend to be sick and agree with me. Now off you go, get dressed, we have to meet an anxious audience. Things will definitely be different," said Edward. Phillip sat on the bed without moving.

"One more thing I want you to bear in mind, I am not King Daniel who thought he could get rid of my sister so easily. I know I will rule this kingdom soon, very soon. There is no one here who is brave enough to stand up to me. I have them eating out of my hands."

He was motionless and spellbound. He began to think about the ball, with Sharon, dancing and singing, and his mother and father laughing. Then being on the chariot fighting for their lives. It was a nightmare.

His entire life changed in front his eyes like a flash. He remembered Sharon and the rose he gave her and promise he made to her.

Sharon gave him the rose saying that they would share everything together and she let him keep it. He found it and kissed it, passing it on his face and began to cry silently. Suddenly he heard footsteps coming closer and closer to his room and loud voices talking anxiously to each other. He hid the rose under the pillow.

He jumped when the door suddenly opened. "Why aren't you dressed as yet, don't waste any more time, didn't you hear what King Edward said?" That was one of the servants. She looked at him with such contempt. Roselyn, why are you doing this?" asked Phillip. "Don't you dare talk back at me or else straight to King Edward. Do you think I want to be a servant forever. No, the new king has offered us handsomely to work for him.

"He told us the incident that took place between your parents and him. Your parents knew about him all along. The kingdom was to be shared between your father and king Edward. He said your father outsmarted him and took everything. King Edward said he had to struggle and fight to survive, and almost nearly gave up his life to save you. He also said that your father even took away your mother from him." Roselyn, that's all lie, how can you believe him."

You know my parents for so long, how can you turn against them so fast." Said Phillip crying. "Don't speak to me in that tone. King Edward is so kind, when he came he said we would not have to work in such conditions anymore, once we believe and care

PG

for him. He agreed to increase our wages and working conditions.

He told me all I have to do is to cook and take good care of you," replied the servant. "Isn't that work Roselyn?" asked Phillip. "It's not the same, he promised a new home and lots of animals and even my own servants. Your parents never cared like that." "That's not true, he's lying to you. All he wants is to rule the kingdom and to gain power so he can govern everything and everyone," shouted Phillip.

"What's going on here?" barged in Edward. "Nothing, your highness, I was just explaining to young Phillip," "explaining what, interrupted Edward harshly. Didn't I tell you not to speak to him, only when I told you to?" "Yes your highness." "Now go downstairs at once and get ready with the other servants to welcome the guests." Roselyn nodded and left. Edward looked at Phillip and said. "Remember when I agree, you agree and nothing else." Edward was a very cold and cruel man. He took a belt and told Phillip to put both his hands out. "Why I didn't do anything." Edward growled at him and said, "do as I say." He grabbed hold of Phillips' hands and hit him on the palms of both hands. Phillip yelled "mother, father." "That's enough," yelled Edward. This pain should last until the meeting ends. Now get dressed and go downstairs."

Edward waited. "Yes sir, say it." "Yes sir," answered Phillip. "This is the way you will address from now on."

There was a lot of commotion in the hall of the kingdom. There were a lot of ministers and people who came near and far and gathered around to listened to the king addressed the people for the first time. When they saw the young Prince there was a sound of awe in the audience and pity because of the recent tragic loss. The special guests went to give him a kiss and hug and give their condolences. "All right, give him air, come, sit Phillip," said Edward. "You are looking wonderful, young prince," said a member of the crowd "Thank God your parents were God loving people." "Yes," cheered the crowd.

"Tell me, King Edward, the young prince is twelve years old, why didn't you crown him king instead of you?" asked his legal guardian. "I so agree with you all, but as you can see the young prince is still so traumatized and shocked, how can he become king if he does not know what is going on, answered Edward.

As you all know the late King and Queen ruled so efficiently and were loved by all their subjects, how could I leave the kingdom unattended like that? Who knows if the murderer will comeback if he knows that the kingdom has no King and Queen. Next thing we know he will want to kill the young prince." Everyone gasped. "Oh, you are so right," they said. "Pardon me your highness," said the legal guardian. "Yes, go on," said Edward. "If what you said is true, do you have it in writing that as soon as the young prince became himself once again you will give him the crown and he will rule?" Edward looked at the crowd.

"That was my first choice, but the young prince was so shaken and could barely spoke, with tears in his eyes when he said he wanted me to protect the kingdom the way I protected him from the murderer," stated Edward. The crowd fell for that and gave a sad sigh to know how Phillip was scared. "Well then I'm sure prince Phillip can sign his name stating that as soon as he is fine he will regain his kingdom," replied the legal guardian. "Of course, I have the papers right here, I will let you read it out loud so that it will please the people," answered Edward. The legal guardian agreed and after reading he handed over the documents to Phillip. Phillip raised his hands and put them on the table.

To their surprise, his hands were red and swollen. "Oh dear," said the legal guardian, please excuse him, he is in so much pain right now. Some things take much longer to heal. The poor lad cannot even bend his fingers. Please let's give him some more time to heal." Edward agreed. "I'm sure with all that swelling you must be in a lot of pain," said Edward. Phillip agreed.

There were sad faces everywhere. Some even began to cry. It was agreed by all that King Edward will rule for now. "Do you want me to rule for now Phillip?" asked Edward. Phillip nodded his head indicating yes. "Then I shall obey your orders to the fullest. Whatever you desire, your wish is my command.

I have grown so fond of him, he is my first priority everything else is secondary." As Edward spoke he did not take his eyes off Phillip, not once. Phillip felt his gaze upon which was enough to scare the daylights out of him. The Ministers looked at his hands closely and said that the wound on his hands looked very fresh. Edward interrupted and said that Phillip needed to be excuse because he has had enough. He addressed the audience one last time. "Thank you all very much for turning up in your numbers. Your presence has shown me how much the royal family has meant to you. Please feel free to meet me anytime if there is a problem. I will continue to serve you to the best of my ability. Thank you for being such loving citizens, good day."

Phillip looked at the swelling in his hands and wanted to speak to the ministers. As he raised his head, he saw Edward in front of him. As he escorted him to his room he spoke to Phillip. "What did the ministers talked to you about." They said to put some medicine on the fingers and hand to avoid further swelling," answered Phillip keeping his head down. Edward looked at him curiously as if he was hiding something then left his room. "I could not sleep Sharon, I thought of you, mother, father and Edward until the wee hours of the morning. I can't remember when I fell asleep. Harry and Smith are my only two friends I can trust to this day."

They both shook their heads and looked at each other very saddened. "I was always sent to my room," continued Phillip. I could not hear anything nor see what was taking place. I had no visitor. Anyone who wanted to see me will have to do so in front of Edward or his servants. He made me rehearsed what I have to say so I will not make a mistake. Many times we fought. I gave him a very hard time. He killed my parents. I could not stand living under the same roof with him but I had no choice.

A number of occasions Harry and Smithy together with some of the servants would help me sneak away from my room to get some fresh air. I will go to places where I spent such happy moments with my parents. The rooms would be dark and gruesome. Some were locked so tight that no one can get in. I would see only dust and cobwebs.

My parents portraits were thrown like thrash in the corner. With these two help I was able to find an abandoned room and placed all my parents valuables and portraits there. They were cleaned and well pollished. I got hold of some of the scrolls before Edward can get his hands on them. Whenever the guards were not looking Harry and Smithy would climbed the walls to my room to meet me.

They both know the kingdom better than I. Whenever I heard commotion outside, I knew one of them has fallen or got caught. This never stopped them. They knew how to talk their way out of difficult situations, even if it does not make any sense. They know every door and corner of the castle. We would draw the doors and corridors. They know every secret passage and they will argue who knows best and who is correct. Of course they will end up fighting. They were my eyes and have hearts of gold, Sharon.

Whatever I want they will provide without any hesitant. They will bring food because what I get to eat did not taste good and the portion was not enough only to keep me alive. On many occasions the cooks were caught stealing fruits and food, but with the help of these two who are very witty of course, they were pardoned. Smithy had a way to the cooks' heart and when he spoke to them they gave him anything he asked for. This was how I spent my early years as a teenager. When I'm distressed and all alone, the memories I had of you at our first meeting was the only hope I had. I was determined to meet you and that was the one and only reason why I stayed alive.

Chapter *Eleven*

I lived like that for years. When I became twenty, I decided to end everything. I was too weak and feeble, but growing up with loved ones I became stronger and stronger to stand up for Edward. He had too many guards, he became very strong. He controlled everyone and they obeyed him. A lot of them were forced to listen to him. They were the loyal subjects to my parents.

I studied him well over those years I was in captivity. I knew his weak points and how he operated. Edward had everything, except one, my signature. You see I was supposed to give my signature to relieve myself from any connections with the kingdom. I was careful not to sign the document in the past with my tricks and scheme. I can also play the game.

I told him when I became twenty, I would give my signature if he would set me free. He agreed instantly because I knew he would kill me instead.

One day he came into my room and said the day has arrived for me to sign. I looked at him for a while and saw a very insecure man who was only interested In wealth and I knew he would kill me. Edward was ignorant of the fact that I knew everything that was happening In the castle. Thanks to my loyal subjects. I said yes that I would do it, under one condition. It must be done on my twentieth birthday. He agreed. Before he left, I asked what reason he would give his people why I handed over everything to him. He said insanity. He told me the people knew that I've become disenchanted in becoming the king.

Edward told the people that I'm a nervous wreck and I live on medicine everyday. He said that they would agree with anything he told them. From then on we all planned how I should escape from the castle. One day as I watched my royal subjects arguing and discussing what is the best way to escape I thank my parents for being such kind and considerate rulers to these people, because it was their hope and prayers that made me escaped. They thought of everything, ensuring me of my safety. Through God's grace their plan worked.

I escaped. I rode without looking back and here I am today looking at you. Some of Edward's soldiers followed me, but I was too swift for them. "That was you they were looking for. I saw them that morning with all that noise and commotion and then suddenly they left. I wondered what was going on, but I had no clue it was you," said Sharon. Sharon laid her head on his shoulder. He held her closer and said, "I've found you once again. Only when I die I will leave you." Sharon smiled and buried her face on his chest. Harry and Smithy were looking and they too hugged each other and wept for joy. "It seems that all our work has paid off, but not quite yet," said Harry.

"Our dear prince has found his true love once again," said Smithy who kept on hugging Harry and would not let go. Harry gave him a shove and he almost fell. "This is our future King and Queen, said Harry. We have a lot of work to do."

Back at Notting Hill castle, Daniel was attending to the vegetable garden with his children. He could feel the presence of Rebecca's stare on him. He gave a sarcastic smile and continued his work. Elizabeth began to sing. She had a celestial voice. Even though she was weak her voice was powerful and vibrant. Rebecca knew she couldn't compete with that. She tried to stop her many times, but failed. She could not stop Daniel and the children from hearing her either. Their mother sang her heart out. The two children held each other and listened.

They looked at each other and smiled. How they looked forward to hearing their mother's voice. It pierced the calmness and went through to their hearts and lingered there for a long while. Daniel closed his eyes and try to take in as much as he could when he heard his darling wife's voice. It brought back memories. That's the key reason she sang so much, to have hope and not despair.

Daniel felt stronger and more alive and realized that this was Elizabeth's weapon against Rebecca. When he raised his head and stood up, he was astonished to see how beautiful the rose garden had become. The roses were bright in color, especially the red ones. Daniel looked at the red roses on the walls of the white castle. The vines were upright and created a heavenly beauty. "Look father, look how beautiful the garden has become," said Louisa, his second daughter.

"It's mothers' singing, isn't it, "replied his son Michael. Daniel looked around the castle as if he has been seeing it for the very first time. "Your mother is telling us to have faith, we will be together again soon." He recollected the moments he shared with his wife.

He remembered the hard work they both did in helping the poor and needed, building bridges with those villagers near and far, attending to their needs and working hand in hand in almost everything they do. He began that work when he threw Rebecca out of the castle so that he can regain the people's faith and trust. When he met Elizabeth they both continued and never stopped. He also made a promise the them that as long as he was king there would be no unnecessary suffering of any kind among his subjects. He allowed them to visit him whenever there was a problem.

Daniel became enraged and that very moment, raised his sword and said, "It is time for me to take back my castle." His voice roared throughout the length and breath of the castle echoing. Rebecca was startled when she heard his voice. She gave a very wicked laugh. What she failed to realized was that they were getting stronger and stronger by just having memories of each other. The love and warmth they shared have instilled in their heart and was very much alive.

Sharon was having the time of her life. Every morning she would leave with a basket full with goodies and told her grand parents she would be back soon, which she never did. They both became concerned about her behavior and that she was hardly home. "Who is responsible for this? Ask her grandmother. She is so happy and full of life. I've never seen her so happy before." "Neither have I," replied Alfred. They were both worried. The next day Sharon told her grandparents that she was bringing a surprise. She was so full of joy, they just stood there and watched her. That evening, Sharon came home early. She came with Prince Phillip.

The grand parents could not believe their eyes when they saw him. That was the first time Sharon brought a boy home. They didn't know how to react, they were speechless. "This is Phillip, my friend who I spend all my free time with. He is the one who has put sunshine and laughter into my life." She turned to Phillip and said. "This is my grandparents who I spoke about so much." "Hello, Sharon speaks so highly of you, I feel that I know you all my life. It is an honor to meet you." "I told him everything, grand mother." "Everything?" she asked unbelieveably." "Yes everything." Her grandmother looked at Alfred and fainted. "Quick, bring some water and put her on the sofa," said Alfred.

When her grandmother awoke, she saw Phillip standing next to her. "I have another surprise for you." Both grandparents became very scared this time. "Grandmother, do you remember a long time ago in the castle a young Prince showed you a ring." "That was too long for me to recollect, dear." "Do you remember the Prince who showed you the ring?" asked Phillip. "I remembered vaguely. It was in my Daniel's castle. He was so proud and bold when he spoke, that cute little Prince."

Phillip continued, "You told me to give it to someone special. Do you remember how the ring looked like?" "I'm sorry son, I can't, why?' asked grandmother. "My dear grandmother, this is the Prince and I am the special one he gave the ring to." "What are you saying, dear?" asked Alfred. "Grandfather, this is Prince Phillip who is supposed to help me break the spell to free my family." They just stood there looking. "That's impossible, replied grandmother in a whispering voice. How can this be, where did you find him?" "It's a long story and you will know every detail after a hearty lunch" replied Sharon.

After listening to them, her grandmother began to cry. "O Sharon I prayed for this day so long and it has finally reached. Thank you Lord, you have given us hope." "Yes indeed, and I will see to it that King Daniel regain his kingdom and all will be well once more," said Prince Phillip.

She rose from her seat and hugged the Prince. "You have grown into a handsome young man." "I think so too," said Sharon and they all smiled. Everyday Phillip, Harry and Smithy would visit them. They helped with the chores around the house. Harry and Smithy attended to the animals so Sharon would spend more time with Phillip. This way everything would look normal to the neighbors. "Her birthday is just around the corner, and I am confident that everything will be all right," said Alfred.

Meanwhile at the castle Daniel with his children were determined to fight for Elizabeth. "Dear God, if I don't regain the kingdom, I pray that you will grant me my wife and kids back. Please unite us once more," prayed Daniel. There was a soft wicked cackle emanating from the castle's wall. Daniel paid no heed to it, because he became accustomed to it.

One day Sharon, Phillip, Harry and Smithy decided to visit the castle. "Please be very quiet, her eyes are everywhere, said Sharon. She can see us, but we can't see her." Phillip's two helpers were scared to death, not knowing what to expect. "Just don't look at the walls, she lives in the walls." "How can someone live in the walls Harry," whispered Smithy with wide eyes opened. "Shh, quiet before she hears us." As they walk pass the rose garden, Sharon saw glances of her childhood. "Give me the compass Phillip, father will tell us which direction to meet him," said Sharon. As Phillip stretched to hand her the compass, he tripped and hurt his ankle.

"Ahh...," he groaned and fell. "Phillip are you allright?" asked Sharon. Harry and Smithy stood motionless, refusing to breathe. "I'm all right, I think I hurt my ankle, help me get up. Well come on, don't be afraid." Both men ran towards and lifted him up. "Lean on me my Lord, I'll carry you," said Smithy.

Daniel was attending to the vegetables with one of the servants when he thought he heard something. He asked the servant, who said no. He listened for a while, and continued to work. Rebecca on the other hand heard Phillip's cry and became alert at once.

She sprang from wall to wall looking out at the castle grounds to see who made that noise, but could see no one. She gave a sigh of relief and forgot about it. It was not time for any visit from the grandparents.

Elizabeth was combing her hair and recollecting the wonderful times she had when she was beautiful. While looking at the mirror, something caught her eyes through the mirror. She saw two figures in the rose garden and was startled. "So soon, I wonder what is the problem, she wondered. Why did father came so soon? Oh I must warm them." She began to sing as loud as she could. Daniel and everyone else heard her. He smiled when he heard her melodious voice. Sharon and the others heard her and Sharon became emotional.

Phillip comforted her. Harry and Smithy were very sad for her. "Your mother has a celestial voice," said Phillip. Her voice echoed throughout the kingdom as if to warm someone. Rebecca was resting when she heard her voice.

Chapter *Twelve*

She opened her eyes a little and then wide. Her body was a shadow and her eyes were red with rage. She was indeed a horror to look at.

While the singing was still going on, that put a smile on Daniel's face. Hearing her voice means that she was fine. He noticed that Elizabeth had never sang that way before. He listened and listened to her words carefully. She repeatedly sang the same words over and over again. He heard her say giving warmth and visiting early a few times. That was strange to him. He heard words like be careful, be alert and cautious. "What is she singing, why is she singing such a sad song?"

He became very worried. "Something is wrong, prepare yourselves," he told everyone. He ran out searching everywhere and realized that she was warning him of something. He didn't know what to do and started to shout. "Take cover, be careful, something is wrong." He carried his children inside the castle and hid them under the stairs. "Be alert children." "Yes father," they replied. Daniel ran back outside, looked around and while running Elizabeth was singing very loudly and not stopping. He then ran towards the garden and stopped.

There he saw Sharon with the rest of them. Harry and Smithy saw him first and were too scared to speak. "My Lord," said Harry with a shaken voice. "There is a man looking at us. At first Phillip did not hear what he said and Harry repeated it. Phillip turned and saw Daniel. "Who is he? asked Smithy. "He is not a ghost, is he Harry?" They were confused.

Sharon turned and yelled, "father, it's me Sharon tell us where to meet you, give us direction." Daniel was so overwhelmed when he heard his daughters 'voice. "Quickly, tell us where to meet you." He was taken back, "this can't be Sharon, she can't be here. She cannot enter the castle grounds for she will die. This is a trick from Rebecca. What is she up to now. "This is what Elizabeth was trying to tell me," he said to himself.

"Father what are you doing, I'm your daughter, Sharon." Daniel was spellbound and could not talk at that moment. The thought of just hurting his own daughter was too much. Sharon thought of Rebecca. "Rebecca, you will try over and over again but I swear you will never succeed." "Who is Rebecca," asked Harry. "She is the woman who live in the walls of the castle."

Father thinks I am her. "King Daniel Sir, I'm Prince Phillip, and this is your daughter Sharon. We came early to see you. Here's the compass, how else can we have this compass if we are not who we say we are. Rebecca cannot leave the castle, remember so she can't possibly be in possession of the compass." "That's true she can't leave," said Daniel. "O father, you looked so frailed and old." "That I am". He looked at her and began to cry. "I can't even recognized my own daughter, what have I become.

He sank on the ground and sobbed. "Don't cry father, we are all here through God's grace." Harry and Smithy were so anxious and spoke at the same time. "The compass, please give direction." "Oh, I forgot father is here we don't need any direction." "Yes,'said Daniel, I am here now, let's go now." They held each other and ran towards the old fountain. They heard laughter, first softly then it became louder and louder filling the entire kingdom with her hoarse voice. "O Daniel, you have made life easier for me once again. So Sharon is here with other guests, how wonderful," growled Rebecca.

Elizabeth was crying her heart out when she saw her husband and daughter reunited again. Harry and Smithy were so scared they hid under a table with their heads down. Sharon introduced Phillip once again with his loyal subjects. She embraced her brother and sister who could not take their eyes off her. Daniel was so pleased to see how beautiful she has grown. "Mother and father have taken good care of you," he said hugging her. The servants came to greet her and bowed. She hugged them so lovingly. There was some joy and merriment in the castle after so many years.

"Now that Rebecca knows that you are here, we have to be on our guard at all times. She will hurt you Sharon every chance she get," said Daniel. "Don't worry Sir, I am ready for her," replied Phillip. He drew his sword. "Your sword is no match for her, son." Rebecca could sense there was someone else with Sharon which troubled her. She knew the visit came early and wondered why.

Prince Phillip was a very brave Prince. He held his sword tighter and kept turning around and looking at everything carefully. Where ever he turned, he could swear he saw someone watching him. This kept on for a while until he realized that someone was playing with his mind. He heard whispers in his ears, sometimes near and then far. He heard laughter and then felt someone passed and touched him. He became more vigilant and was ever more ready. Rebecca was having fun with him. "You are indeed a Prince, so brave and full of life, but you are no match for me, what a pity," she spoke to her herself.

"Sharon, did you bring the compass?" "Yes father." "Good, I have something to show you." Phillip came to join them, they were all curious to know what Daniel had to say. "This compass has something that no one else know except my parents and Elizabeth." "What good will that do?" asked Michael, his son. Daniel continued, "where's my sword." "I'll go get it." "No, said Daniel, just say where it is." "It's under the stairs." "Watch carefully, just step aside and don't move especially not in front of me." Smithy and Harry eyes were wide opened as they looked on, there was a hidden magnet on the compass. Daniel faced the magnet on the compass to where the sword was hidden. Suddenly, out of no where the sword came with a speed faster than anyone can imagine right towards Daniel who grabbed it before it can attacked him. Sharon screamed, "father look out." Smithy fell to the ground followed by Harry. "What's this, how did you, what magic is this?" asked Phillip. Daniel said smiling, "this my boy is our ticket out of here. This magnet can pull anything that has a magnetic field on it as far as the eyes can see."

When the two loyal subjects were up they heard Daniel said that the sword is one of its kind and is very special. "It's not just a sword, look at it carefully." "I don't see anything different in it, father," said Sharon. "Well my dear, every engrave you see in the sword means there is a spear inside." "You mean there are ten small spears on this sword?" asked Phillip. "You are so right, I will show you," said Daniel.

"You see, when you are under attack and are surrounded, you hold the sword in the position you want. He raised the sword at arms' length. Watch where I put my hand." Everyone was still and looked on. Daniel pressed a knob and lo and behold, ten small knives like spears shot out of the sword like arrows towards the target Daniel was facing it. On seeing this everyone ran for cover. They were shocked.

"This is amazing, I've never seen anything like this in my entire life," answered Phillip with eyes wide opened. He was about to touch it, when Daniel stopped him. "It is sharper than anything you have ever came across." It is very dangerous. This sword can cut through your hand like paper." "I don't doubt you sir," said Harry. "This sword is the only weapon that can stand up to Rebecca. Once they are released they will return to where they belong." Said Daniel. "How amazing, it's unbelievable," said Sharon.

At that moment, they all heard Elizabeth's voice calling through the air like a goddess. She sang a very sad song. They could not understand all the words, but the way she sang they knew she was troubled. "O mother, I missed you so much," said her daughter Louisa. "We all missed her tremendously, but now is not the time to get emotional dear.

We all have to be brave for each other. Together we can kill Rebecca," answered Sharon. "You said it, my love," replied Phillip. Rebecca was uneasy because she knew Sharon was in the castle. "I underestimated you, you worm," as she paced up and down thinking what to do next.

Elizabeth looked at herself in the mirror. How she longed to be strong again so that she could joined the others to fight Rebecca. She was saddened to know that her loved ones are risking everything just for the family to be reunited. That feeling sickened her more and she kept looking at herself crying. She saw a frail, old woman with a few strands of long hair combed in braid. She missed her life with her children so much. She put her hands on her face and wept bitterly. She began to pray, "My God, please give me the strength to carry on, I don't care what happened, but I will fight for my love ones to the very last.

"Now listen up, Rebecca can move from wall to wall. She cannot stay out of the walls for long because of the curse. "Daniel turned to the servants and said, "you will behave the same as if nothing is going on. I know Rebecca will look at you all to know what is going on. Rebecca normally stays near Elizabeth's chamber guarding her, therefore she resides on the walls surrounding her chamber. That's the chamber right under the roof where she can see the entire castle all around. Sometimes, through your mother's singing she will tell me where Rebecca is located. She will guide me so that I will not be seen. This is how we communicated all these years," said Daniel.

Elizabeth began to sing once again. "See, she is telling us that there is a storm approaching," said

Daniel. "How interesting," said Phillip, as they entered the back entrance of the castle into the kitchen. They tried their best not to stumble or make any noise what so ever. "The only way to kill her Is when she is changing walls, we have to be very swift to kill her then. She can destroy us whenever she likes, hope she does not get the chance," said Daniel. Suddenly, the place was slowly becoming dark.

"Hurry, hide she is coming," The servants became busy, one began to hum a tune. Rebecca crept downstairs gliding with her witch behaviours, lurking at every corner paying attention to the servants. She saw nothing different or strange, and went back the same way she came. The servants were relieved becaused they all were afraid of her. "I thought I was going to die Harry, said Smithy, I could hardly breathe." Phillip patted him on the back and said, "our job has just begun." The two loyal subjects looked at each other scared stiff. "She will not be down here again which will give us some time to go up the stairs." Said Daniel. As they kept climbing the stairs, keeping close to each other Sharon kept looking at the rooms and hallway and remembered how wonderful it was once.

Chapter *Thirteen*

Phillip saw her and hugged her reassuring her that it will happen again. She remembered her childhood days. She had her hair down with a clip keeping it together. As the sun seeped through the castle and fell on her hair, it glowed so brightly it filled the place with brilliance.

This brilliance reached the eyes of Rebecca. When she saw the hallway getting brighter than usual, she began to investigate. She thought it was just the sun rays. As the family moved towards the rooms going up the sun followed them. Sharon's hair glowed like never before, which added so much light in the rooms. There was one more flight of stairs to meet Elizabeths' when suddenly out of nowhere thunder strike. That startled everyone. Harry almost fell on the floor and yelled for Smithy to help him. Smithy beckoned him to be quiet. "I don't want to die," said Harry. "No one is going to die," answered Phillip who ran and held his hand. "Thank you your highness," said Harry. "Well, she was right as usual, here comes the storm.

Rebecca loved stormy weather, with very dark clouds and thunder and lightning. Then something happened that no one suspected. As the sun was no more Sharon's hair continued to glow and reflected on the walls of the castle. Rebecca was not far from them at all. She noticed the difference on the shades on the walls, but did not heed. She looked at the storm approaching.

She was pleased to see the place getting darker and darker inside and outside. As she headed back to her domain, she was startled by the ray of light coming from the walls a distance away. She moved without it walking, like a ferocious cat ready to pounce on its' prey. As she turned the corner she was startled by the mirror on the far end of the corridor. What did she see. There in the mirror she saw the back of Sharon's hair.

She blinked her eyes over and over again. She tried to get away from the glare. As she looked in the mirror, she looked at her own strand of hair which belonged to Sharon. As Rebecca stroke the strand, it suddenly became fuller and healthier. "Yes, yes, said Rebecca, she is very close now isn't she," and laughed. Sharon felt as if someone had touched her and turned around. All she could see was a tall black figure with a shriek of golden hair just disappeared into the wall. At that moment Sharon knew it was her. That was the very first time she laid eyes on Rebecca. A bit of fear came over her, but she was determined to fight for her mother, if it meant taking her last breath away from her. Phillip saw her breathing heavily and comforted her. "I think we are very close now," said Daniel.

The corridors became darker and darker and colder and colder which indicated that Rebecca resided there. "Here is where she is staying at the moment. When they touched the walls, they were sticky and icy cold. They got a weird feeling when they touched the walls. They felt like there was life in them. All they heard is light breathing coming from them. "I think we should stay very close together and not touched these walls, said Daniel.

Rebecca will feel our touch through them." She did indeed. She knew exactly where they were and as she approached them, out of the cold darkness, there came a heavenly celestial voice of Elizabeth. As she sang to guide them as to where to go, Rebecca froze because her voice illuminated the corridor. Rebecca suddenly vanished into thin air.

Sharon cried out, "mother," and ran towards her voice. Phillip grabbed her hand and whispered to her. "All we can do now it to follow her voice. She is leading us to her and is keeping us safe as well. Don't do anything foolish."" Sharon was so anxious. "She is fine isn't she, I just know it," she said. "I hope so," replied Daniel. "We must have a plan. We will distract Rebecca and find Elizabeth at the same time.

He looked at the sword and said. "Listen up, when I release the sword in the direction where Rebecca should be, I want you to open the door that comes in front of you. When you don't see your mother come back as quickly as you can without touching the walls, you hear me?' said Daniel looking at his last two children. "Yes, father," they said. They listened to Elizabeth's voice. As she sang she indicated that three doors away the witch will be resting, take heed for she is waiting.

Rebecca was so outraged to hear that. Daniel raised the sword and aimed as far as he could and hoped that he could hit the wall after the three doors where she was resting. He released with such power and zest. The little arrows hit the walls with such screeching noise, it scared the hell out of everyone. Harry and Smithy remain spellbound and couldn't even scream. "Run, said Daniel, find your mother."

They all went with such haste scampering from door to door and screaming mother. "She's not here father," said Sharon. "Keeping looking." Everyone yelled for her. "She is no where to be found and there are no more doors," said Phillip. "Come back, come back," Daniel shouted. They all came back out of breath and frightened. "We didn't see her," they all talked at once. The children tried to keep the tears from flowing. We tried out best, the rooms were dark and deserted," said Smithy. "That was our first try, don't worry, she will tell us something again," answered Daniel.

Rebecca felt the children's touch on the walls as they came back. She was about to laugh but was stopped abrupt. It was her body. You see wherever the blades scratched the walls they actually were on Rebecca's body instead. Her eyes were opened as large as can be. She could not believe what she saw. There were so many cuts and bruises on her entire body she began to scream. She screamed and screamed with her eyes as red as blood. Her screams sounded like screeches instead. She was so outraged, she flew into the air like a twister and down again. Everyone held their hands on their ears.

The children buried their heads on their father. The sound was unbearable. Smithy made the sign of the cross and said his time had come. As Michael kept breathing heavily, he heard a dripping sound on the walls. When he looked carefully he saw blood dripping from the walls. He thought he did not see clearly. He took a closer look.

"Father, he stuttered with fear, look over here."

What is it my son?" The walls are bleeding." They all froze. Smithy almost fainted and replied. "What evil is this?" She lived in the walls, therefore she is apart of them and where ever the blades strike, they were actually striking her.

"Do you know my Lord, the witch is wounded?" said Harry. "Yes, yes of course, and is badly wounded as well," said Sharon.

Daniel took a long look, and where ever the blades strike blood keep dripping. This meant that she was seriously hurt. They all breathe a sigh of relief. While resting they heard her screamed once again. This alerted them once more. "It will take a very powerful person to conquer her," said Daniel.

Something happened out of the ordinary. Rebecca was a very skilled witch who practiced black magic to its capacity. As they looked at the walls, they saw something that caused their eyes to almost pop out. They heard Rebecca saying." As you enter my body with a rush so you will come out with a rush bringing back every drop of blood you spilled." She spoke in such a dreadful voice. Her eyes became red and fiery, and hair stood on end as she chanted the spell.

They all looked at the walls watching the blood going back into the walls, not leaving a trace of blood left. Even the blood on the sword vanished.

They all watched in horror. As the blood left the walls, the scratches on them began to close in and healed themselves. As this happened, there was a screeching sound so horrifying and painful, they all closed their ears and screamed. That happened until all the scratches were closed in. They all heard her sigh and knew that she was back to normal. Everyone was on the floor, too weak to stand.

They held on to each other tightly so that no one would touched the walls. It was a desperate situation. They looked at each other not knowing what to do. Phillip kept looking at the walls where the blood flow and studied it. At one time he got the urge to touch it. When he did it felt warm. He didn't want to believe it, and then he touched it again. That time his fingers went a bit through it. It felt as if he was touching someone. "Rebecca," he murmured. He now fully understood who he was dealing with. He began to breathe slowly and heavily studying her and thinking what to do next.

Once again Elizabeth began to sing. Her voice was closer than before, which means she was nearer than before. "Be patient but cautious, you are on the right direction." When Rebecca heard that, she began to move from wall to wall faster and faster to distract them.

Chapter *Fourteen*

They saw the shadow and laid on the floor so she could not see them. They were still, fearing not to breathe for she might hear them. They all saw her in the wall. A horrible creature with a shriek of golden hair. "That's the hair she took from you Sharon. That's what keeping her strong and ahead of us. She is living through your strength." "I know that father," she said. Rebecca became so uneasy, she flew from wall to wall grunting and moving very swiftly as if to confuse them. The walls looked like they were moving sometimes. They had an awful stench and Daniel knew that Elizabeth was very close by.

The corridors became more and more untidy as they move forward listening to Elizabeth's voice. "This is the abode of a witch and is guarding my wife," said Daniel. There was dead silence. Daniel gave a sign of continued silence. They knew anytime now Rebecca would appear in front of them. Sharon listened attentively so that she would not miss a sound. She beckoned everyone to move forward with light footsteps.

As she turned around, she saw Rebecca flying towards them with a high pitch laughter that could kill anyone. She was coming right at them with such speed. They all screamed, even Sharon, who covered her face. But then again, something strange happened. As Sharon was scared enough to see Rebecca, Rebecca too was agast to see Sharon, and vanished at once.

Sharon remained there for a while, waiting for her to strike them. They waited still covering themselves. Nothing happened. Sharon raised her head and saw nothing. She looked at her hands, feet and entire body and nothing happened to her. She was puzzled and hugged herself. She turned around and could see the corridor lit up. Her hair looked so full and long with golden lights on them. Phillip ran his hands through her hair and it remained glowing. "Sharon, your hair is glowing," "Yes, I know." "This is why she fled, she is afraid of you.

You are the light. She is afraid of you, because you are what she is not. You have a pure heart and is the source of everything that is good. Rebecca is the total opposite. You are her rebel," said Daniel. "That means we can defeat her, right father?" asked Michael. "You said it my boy." Daniel's voice had strength and power as he spoke. As her hair began to darken Sharon realized that Rebecca was far away from them.

As they moved forward, they came to a turning point where the corridors were in opposite directions. As they started to move on one direction, they heard a sad sigh from Elizabeth which caused them to choose the other. Elizabeth can take care of herself after all these years she kept herself alive. "It is you Sharon, that Rebecca is interested in. If she kills you, we are all doomed. She needs to kill you and can hear your heart beat, said Daniel. She is connected to you by that strand of your hair in her head. You two are connected. "I've got a plan, said Daniel.

Since Rebecca is afraid of you Sharon, you should continue to search for her to distract her. This will make it easy for us to find Elizabeth. Once she is with us, we can fight her together." "Yes father, I will do just that." "My Lord, may I say something, said Harry to Phillip. "I would like Smithy and myself to accompany her. This is too much for her alone." Philip was overwhelmed. My loyal subjects are sacrificing their lives for his happiness. "No, not at all, interrupted Sharon. I can handle this without putting you both at risk." Daniel was so grateful for their wonderful gesture.

"My two fine gentlemen, thank you from the bottom of my heart for wanting to do this, but I think you will slow down Sharon, she can manage perfectly. I know this or else I would have never allowed it. There was silence once again. Sharon listened attentively and then said in a whispering voice so that Rebecca could hear her. "I am going to look for mother, stay back all of you." She took a different route hoping Rebecca will follow her. As she kept walking and looking at the walls to see if she saw any shadow or anything, but nothing. She kept looking at her hair to see any glow, but nothing.

As she walked further and further down the corridor she realized something. Rebecca was not afraid of the others but her. That meant she would go after them and not her. She would not be there to protect them. "O no, what have I done, my family." She turned and began to run as fast as she could. As she ran she started calling out to Phillip, but he did not respond. Suddenly, she saw them. When she called out they did not answer. As she came closer she knew something was wrong. Rebecca got her claws on all of them including Elizabeth. "Oh, what have I done mother." "Don't worry my darling, I still have life in me yet," said her mother.

Rebecca laughed and the castle shook. The servants trembled with fright and were so concerned about the royal family. "Have you not heard that walls have ears Sharon? she replied," I can enter this room only when your sweet mother was concentrating on her loved ones.

When she saw them she left her guard down and here I am. I can kill them all this instant as we speak. Who do you want me to kill first, your choice. Your wish is my command." "Please, please leave them alone. I'll do anything you ask, anything." "Well well, then I might just have a proposition for you." "No Sharon," shouted Daniel. "Don't listen to her, save yourself, it is you she really want. Once you are alive, we will always have hope.

As Daniel spoke, Rebecca raised her hand and threw him across the room. "Oh Daniel, said Elizabeth, are you alright." She ran towards him. "Remember the curse honey, you are not to touch me or look at me." "I remembered Daniel," she answered. Sharon was so hurt to see her family suffering so much. She straightened herself and said to Rebecca. "Whatever do you want, I will do it."

Her mother tried to stop her but failed. "Now that is much better, I'm a very considerate person. I will not ask for much. All I want is your hair, and I will set everyone free. "No Sharon," said Daniel as he beckoned Sharon to look down the corridor where Harry and Smithy were with the sword. Sharon saw them.

"I will give you all my hair once you set them free.

I will cut off my hair and give it to you." She took the scissors from the draw and cut off her hair. Rebecca became excited and anxious. "Give it to me, give it to me." Here you are Rebecca, enjoy. Sharon threw the hair on the wall of the castle. She spread her hair from wall to wall and on the floor.

Rebecca screamed as the hair fell all over the palace. For her to collect all the hair, she had to come out of the wall and collect it as a person. As she did so Harry and Smithy were waiting for her.

Harry raised the sword and released the arrows where ever he saw Rebecca. The arrows hit the wall and missed her. Then hit again and struck her. She was in pain and screamed. Harry aimed again trying to control the sword so that it will hit the target. The knives missed her once again. Rebecca was hurt as she was hit twice. Phillip was with Sharon and the kids were with their mother. Rebecca's screams fainted and all was quiet again.

As Harry aimed to the walls where the knives fell they all came flying back to the sword. They knew she has taken her real form and was out of the walls. Sharon's hair was scattered everywhere. Suddenly it began to glow. The corridor was lit up. In the distance they heard Rebecca's scream. They knew she was badly hurt. "I am not seeing any blood," said Louisa.

Phillip said, "if Rebecca is hurt, then her mind will be distracted from us especially the queen. It means the spell should not be so strong again. I want to look at you my queen." "No, no, I don't want to hear of it."

As Elizabeth spoke she looked at herself and noticed that she began to change. Her body became a bit stronger and she felt a little stronger herself. As she called out to Daniel she noticed that her voice has become more powerful. "What is it dear?" he asked. "He is right, Phillip is right, I am getting younger. Please don't look everyone. I think the spell has weakened a bit."

"That spell has nothing to do with me. I was nowhere when she did this, therefore I think I can look at you my queen." "Phillip please don't, I don't want anything to happen to you," said Sharon. "The only way to know is to take a quick glance at her." "Please be careful, your highness," said Harry and Smithy shaking with fear. Phillip decided to look at her through the mirror. He straightened himself and turned towards the mirror with his eyes closed. He opened his eyes, took a quick glance and walked away. "Well did you see her?" asked Sharon.

"Yes I saw her. She is wearing a old red gown and has her hair is in a long braid." "That's correct," said Elizabeth. They all waited to see what was going to happen to Phillip. Nothing happened. They hugged each other and laughed. "O Daniel, said Elizabeth, I feel so much stronger now."

"Phillip, you will stay with Elizabeth and the rest of us will head for the corridors," said Daniel.

Elizabeth sank to the ground and said "Rebecca is coming, be prepared." As they listened they heard a windy sound approaching, getting closer and closer and stronger. It came so strong that they held their head, but to no avail. The wind came crashing down through corridor. They saw Sharon's hair came together and just stood on air as Rebecca came closer and closer to collect it. The wind began to subside as Rebecca came in front of them. She was dressed in a black gown. Her hair was black with a strand of gold at the side of her face. Her eyes were large and red in color and her lips were red. Her hair stood on end. It look stiff. She looked at all of them and said. "I under estimated you but all games are over now." As she stretched to hold Sharon's hair which was floating in the air, Phillip grabbed the sword from Harry and aimed at her hand and then her body. She did not screamed that time but looked at him and came closer.

"You, you want to kill me, no one can kill me. You will never live to marry Sharon." "Don't count on it you witch," said Sharon. As Rebecca raised her hand to curse him, Sharon grabbed the floating hair and as she did so it began to glow once again. Rebecca screamed and hid her face. She suddenly began to laugh. She pointed her hand at Elizabeth and began to turn it. Elizabeth began to mourn and grown with pain. "Mother, mother, please don't hurt her," said the children.

Phillip got hold of Sharon with her hair and pushed her to her mother. "Don't look at Sharon, keep the hair with you and hold your mother." As Sharon did this, this confused Rebecca. "How can this be?" she asked. "They cannot see her but they touch her, especially with the glowing hair," said Phillip. Rebecca could not look because of the glowing hair and turned away. She could not cause pain to Ellsabeth anymore. Sharon knew that once she was with her mother Rebecca cannot touch her.

"Mother, listen to me, I know you are very weak, but I know you can do this. After all, you are the one who taught us to be strong and use what God has given us." "O my dear child, I have a strong mind and I can do whatever you want me to do." "I know mother, but I need a strong body as well. You will hold on to me and I will carry you to the rest of the guys O.K." Elizabeth nodded. Rebecca went looking for the others to destroy them. All they could see was a pair of red demonic eyes coming towards them. They all fringed because they knew they don't stand a chance. As she raised her hand and began to cast her spell, Sharon spoke. "Think twice before you leap Rebecca." She turned around and saw Sharon with her mother.

Chapter *Fifteen*

"Don't look at her, close your eyes everyone, she is fine."
Phillip smiled contently. "I'm fine everyone, keep your
eyes shut. Thanks to Sharon I can see you all." Tears
ran down her cheeks. "My poor babies, I love you all
so very much. Daniel, my dear, we have come thus far,
keep your hopes up again and don't despair." "I never
did my darling," said Daniel. The corridor was filled
with so much love at that moment. They heard a thug
and saw Rebecca's shadow fell to the ground at the edge
of the wall.

Her shadow tried to get up but was in a lot of pain.
She had difficulty in getting up. She began to mourn
and then vanished. "That's strange, she seems to have
lost her powers," said Michael. "Indeed she has, my boy.
You see, she is so full of evil that where ever there is love
Rebecca don't stand a chance. Her life is full of anger,
hate, greed and everything negative," replied Daniel.

They all shut their eyes tightly and held on the
Elizabeth. "It's a pleasure to have finally met you my
queen," said Harry with Smithy nodding. She looked
at them with such loving smile.

"Sharon, as your hair keeps glowing Rebecca
cannot hurt us which gives me an idea," said Phillip.

Rebecca became very weak. She tossed and turned on the floor not knowing what happened. Phillip knew that the hair will continue to glow because Sharon was with her entire family, something she never had for a very long time. He also knew that Elizabeth would become stronger and stronger by the minute once she was with her family.

Suddenly, he got a cold shiver and did not understand why Rebecca was with them again. They waited to see what was her next move. Phillip studied her carefully and looked up. There she was looking down at all of them. "Be calm everyone, she can't come any closer, this is as far as she goes," said Phillip. "You think you have all the answers don't you boy." They all jumped whey they heard her voice coming from behind Phillip. "Please everyone, get close to Sharon. Feel for each other and don't let go," said Phillip. They all did as they were told. "You should have used your brain to save your kingdom, but instead you ran away from my brother so you escaped. How heroic of you.

I am much stronger than Edward and much more powerful than him," she said shouting. "She will be back soon, you can count on that," said Smithy.

"Sharon, you must stay amongst us. She cannot come close to us once you are here. She is trying her very best to destroy us but can't because of you," said Phillip. "I love you all very much and I will die but not leave you," she replied. "So Edward is her brother, wait till I get my hands on him," said Daniel clenching his fist. Phillip stopped him. "We need to concentrate and put all our efforts to kill Rebecca now or never." The place became dead silent, not a sound was heard anywhere. "Sharon, we will have to keep moving until we are out on the grounds." She agreed. As they kept moving, they came to a spot where the sunlight was on the corridor. Then they heard a screeching sound that was getting louder and louder.

"Now hold hands and don't let go," said Daniel. "What's that father?" asked Louisa. "Sounds like a large bird and here it comes duck everyone," shouted Daniel. The sound was so piercing, that Louisa began to scream. "Don't be afraid, I got you," and he comforted her. "This is one of her dirty tricks, she is desperate now." "Desperate am I, I'll show you desperate." "O my God what now," said Smithy. They listened silently, trying hard to hear anything. Then it came. "What's that," said Michael.

"The floor, it's coming from the floor, quick the sword," said Phillip. It was too late. What they saw was a slithering figure becoming larger and larger towards them with full speed ahead with blood red eyes looking directly at them. "Don't let go, whatever you do don't let go, hold on to your mother and Sharon," yelled Daniel. Rebecca transformed herself into a huge snake that almost had the size of the corridor.

They all screamed as it was their last. Then there was silence. Once again the corridor was filled with a groaning sound. "Is everyone allright." No one answered. "Please open your eyes and look at each other and not mother." They saw that nothing was wrong with any of them. "What happened?" asked Harry struggling to speak. "This is impossible, the snake came right at us and nobody got hurt, we are all alive," said Daniel. "I know, said Sharon. Mother was the only one not screaming. You see father while we were screaming our heads off, I felt someone cut my hair and saw it fell on the ground. As it remained glowing the snake could not pass and just disappeared," replied Sharon.

"I always carry a pair of scissors with me." O Elizabeth, you always know what to do. You saved us all,' said Daniel. "I told you my mind is still strong," she answered. "Rebecca tried the floor and air but failed to destroy. Now she will try the walls, please be on the alert and don't look at Elizabeth come what may," said Daniel.

"How long are we going to suffer like this," said Smithy shivering with fright. "We don't know what she is up to, we just have to be vigilant," said Phillip trying to console him. They all began to walk slowly and shielded each other. "We have to get hold of Rebecca's hair and cut the golden strand that is Sharons'. I'm sure that strand of hair is sustaining her. She is living because of Sharon and she knows that Sharon has become part of her. That's why she wants Sharon dead," said Phillip.

Rebecca knew, once her hair was cut it would be the end for her. At the far distance they heard a sigh. Sharon's hair glowed enough for them to see where they were going. They knew she was up to something evil, but what. To their surprise they noticed that the corridor was cleaner. As they continued the corridor looked cleaner and cleaner. Daniel stopped followed by everyone. There was silence. "Why did she leave her resting place. What caused her to do this." They looked at each other. "Of course it's a trap," said Phillip. "Maybe it's the hair that caused it." "What do you mean?" asked Sharon. "Rebecca saw your hair on the ground and she must have thought that it is all over for her, not knowing that it is just part of your hair that is cut off. This caused her to become disillusioned and she took the wrong turn. That is the only answer I have," said Daniel." "That's it, that's it," said Phillip. It means she cannot find her way back.

"What we have to do is find her. She will be very quiet if possible. She knows that she is lost because of the light. She feeds on darkness." They walked very slowly and tried not to make a breath. Elizabeth decided to let everyone rest for a while. While sitting on the floor they heard her. It was a rather strange sound. It was difficult to say what it was. First Phillip said it sounded like scratching on the wall, then Sharon said it sounded like something was dragging and walking. "All right all right calm down, said Elizabeth. Let's put all the sound together and figure what it is. They began to walk slowiy towards it and came to an intersection. Daniel recognized the place and knew that those were his childrens' room.

The sound was coming from the opposite direction. As they turned and looked, they were all stunned to see a very ferocious eagle walking towards them. It's eyes were blood red and had a long horrible beak. As it walked the huge wings scratched the walls and the back of the eagle was dragging as it walked. They all held their breadth and stood motionless afraid to even blink. The eagle looked disoriented and depressed. As it raised it's head and saw them, the eyes opened wide with rage and flew towards them. As it flew it made a most horrifying sound that scared the daylights out of them. They held their heads and screamed while running away from it.

That screeching sound was heard throughout the length and breadth of the village. "What evil is this cried Martha," and held on to Alfred. The villagers were taken aback and started to run for shelter. The servants ran for cover where ever they could find. Some knelt down and began to pray. They believed that was the end for the royal family. The noise was unbearable. As the eagle flew the wings were grazing the walls which caused them to fall on the ground. The children began to cry and Daniel comforted them.

Harry and Smithy fell on their knees and held their ears. The screeching continued for a while together with the grazing of the wings on the walls echoed throughout the kingdom. Before it reached them, Phillip yelled. "Sharon, you are our only hope. Let your hair glow as it has never glowed before. This is the only way Rebecca can die. Think of all your loved ones and save us please.

While running Sharon thought of her life with her grandparents, her family and the love of her life Phillip. She felt very warm and love inside. Her hair began to glow brighter and brighter. It shone so bright that it almost blinded everyone in the corridor. Rebecca began to fly high and low hitting the walls and swaying to and fro. Then there was an abrupt silence. They all remained still and refused to move. Daniel spoke. "Is everyone all right?' he asked. He heard no answer. "Please check the person next to you and speak up" To their surprise no one was injured. This puzzled them so much. "Look everyone, Rebecca has turned into her true self.

She was a sight to see indeed. Her gown was torn and covered with blood. Her arms and face were badly bruised and were dripping with blood. Even her head was bleeding. She was sitting in a pool of her own blood. She moved very slowly feeling her way to get up. She tried and fell again.

Daniel gave a sign for everyone to be silent. "The light has blinded her for now. She does not know where she is. We have to be extremely quiet. This is our chance or else we will be all doomed." "Sharon, she has a piece of hair that is keeping her alive. We need to get that out of her," said Phillip. "I have the scissors with me," replied Elizabeth. "How do we get close to her without letting her know it is us?" asked Daniel. "We must have a plan soon before she came to her senses." Elizabeth suggested that they all lured her towards them and one of them would cut off the hair. "That's my job said Sharon, I'll do it." Everyone insisted that it is their job. Harry and Smithy insisted that they can do it.

Chapter *Sixteen*

"We are your humble servants, it is an honor to serve you my Lord," said Harry looking at Phillip. He embraced them lovingly and said "Thank you, but Sharon is my responsibility, I will do it." "The hair in Rebecca's hair is mine, no one is leaving but me. "Before Phillip could respond Elizabeth intervened and said that Sharon was right. "She is afraid of you most. You are her rebel my child. Today this ends, it is either we all live or die together." "Sharon, my darling you are my rock and my first born. You have grown to become a powerful and strong young woman.

You are full of beauty both inside and out. I'm very proud of you my child," said Daniel embracing her. "Scissors please," she said and Elizabeth handed it to her. They hugged each other so passionately for a while and slowly let go. With a smile on her face she said. "let's do this." Daniel signaled everyone and began to talk. "Sharon, I am so weak, I need to rest," He spoke in a very painful way. Rebecca heard him and turned to their direction. She leaned her head on the wall for support and listened. "Lean on me father, I can see an entrance, yes it is the sun. Everyone let's go as quickly as we can," said Sharon. Rebecca held on to the walls as she began to walk as fast as she can.

Her feet were badly bruised as she kept falling and getting up. "My feet has no life please help me to walk Sharon, said Phillip. I have to wake my feet," and he started to jump and stumped his feet on the ground so that Sharon can run towards Rebecca. "I can't let them reach the end of the corridor, it will be dangerous for me," said Rebecca. They all began to speak at once talking about themselves, how painful they feel and made a lot of noise so that Sharon can run towards her. As Rebecca held the wall Sharon had enough space to run and held her with one snap. She cut the hair off her head leaving only her black hair on her.

Rebecca groan and screamed her heart out as if her life was over. That scream was music to their ears. They all ran towards her and dragged her until they find a window and threw her out into the sunlight. Sharon threw her hair out the window spreading it on the kingdom. Where ever it fell the place became bright and full of life.

Everything started to blossomed and spring up. The roses began to bloom. The trees looked fuller and strong once again, and before you know it the entire kingdom became alive again. The bees and butterflies made a symphony of sound. The sun shone brighter and the castle began to change into a heavenly place once again. The guards looked for Rebecca everywhere, but she could not be found. Daniel ordered them to search the villages nearby, go into the forest, but to no avail. Three days passed and she was nowhere to be found. All they saw was a trail of dried grass leading towards the river. They assumed that she fell and died.

As Elizabeth heard of her death, they all gathered around her to remove her vail from her face slowly. As she opened her eyes her entire body became young and beautiful as ever.

Her hair became full and golden like her daughter. She was stunning to look at. "O Elizabeth, I've found you once again," said Daniel. Harry and Smithy bowed down and said," your highness." She looked at Phillip and said," welcome to our family and hugged him.

Edward was a much more vengeful wizard than Rebecca. He showed no mercy for anyone. When Prince Phillip arrived, he saw his people working as slaves around the castle. He could hardly recognize some of them. The old, young and even the sick did their part in order to live. He accompanied with Harry, Smithy and soldiers made haste towards his castle. In no time Edward was caught. Prince Phillip took his kingdom and brought peace and harmony once again. It was said that Edward escaped from the dungeon with the help of his guards. Some said that he then drank a glass of water which had poison. He was nowhere to be found. The search lasted over a long period of time until it became hopeless. The prince knew that Edward had a lot of help from his loyal subjects to escape. The guards were afraid to go against his wishes.

The kingdom was filled with laughter and merriment. The fountains were magnificent and roaring with water. The people near and wide came to visit him yes King Daniel of Notting Hill. What a beautiful name, what a beautiful sight to see the King wearing his crown and his entire attire. He looked magnificent indeed. A most handsome man with a warm and loving smile on his face as he watched his people waiting for his speech. There was an uproar when they saw Elizabeth making her entrance to join the king. "My people of Notting Hill, I present to you the King and Queen of Notting Hill.

Everyone jumped and screamed for joy. Balloons were sent up, doves were set free and confetti streamers were blown everywhere, What a site it was indeed. Martha and Alfred held the children with Prince Phillip. They were all so very happy.

Daniel raised his hand and the noise ceased at once. He looked at everyone and took a deep sigh. "I prayed so hard for this day to become a reality. As you know I suffered for eight long years together with my queen, two kids and my loyal subjects. My eldest child was separated from us. She was raised by my loving parents until this day. I am most certainly blessed to have you two for my parents, he said looking at them so lovingly. They took away a very large burden from me when Sharon went to live with them. I felt so satisfied knowing my daughter were with you two. Words cannot describe how grateful I am right now.

All I can do was to pray and thank God to give you health and strength and for you to live for me to see when this day arrives, and here you are in front of me. Thank you Lord. Tears came to the eyes of his parents. Over these past eight years, under the pressure and torment and believe me there were a lot, I never stop thinking of you the citizens on Notting Hill. Thinking of you gave me hope and an inner strength that I never lose all because of you. You have always shown me respect and kindness. You made my life wonderful the best way you can. You stood by me through thick and

thin. You never failed me. You were always with me."
There was an uproar of cheers.

He waited for the crowd to be silent then proceed. "Today my life is so full of joy and happiness and it all because of my good work I've done with you all. My wife suffered silently, my children suffered with me and Sharon suffered the separation from her family. The one hope we had to overcome this dilemma was the love we have for each other. We believed in each other. We fought for each other. We gave up our lives for each other, and here we are today together once again as if nothing had separated us. Thank you my beloved for believing in me.

To you my citizens, my life is complete now that I'm your king once again. I give my love and support to my family, I give my life to you.. The crowd went wild when they heard this. We will continue to work together through thick and thin and bring back the entire city to a more rich an happy place through God's grace, Amen," said King Daniel. "I want to officially welcome my future son-in-law Prince Phillip to the royal family and to you my people.

There were cheers of joy and merriment. He called upon Sharon and her future husband and placed the crowned upon her head once again. "It will always remain there my dear," said Queen Elizabeth. Sharon's friends came to congratulate her. They were so happy to see her and Prince Phillip. They had so many things to tell her. As the royal family made their way out, everyone bowed to them with pride and content. The villager brought whatever stock they had to add with the merriment. The wedding took place a week after and everyone was invited.

Rebecca who disguised herself as a peasant came to bid them farewell. As she saw Princess Sharon and Prince Phillip approached the royal chariot, she could not take her eyes off them. She watched as the couple kissed each other as they entered the chariot. How elegant they both looked. Rebecca had a smile on her face. It was not a happy one nor was it out of contempt. She was sad and her eyes yearned to be like Sharon, to be with the person she loved. She wanted to have a family just like Daniel's, but failed. The chariot sped off and the villagers threw rice and flowers as it went. They both waved at the people on the road side. Rebecca was not in black at all. She wore very bright and colorful attire so no one could recognized her.

Looking on at the edge of the forest was someone else who was not invited. He was dressed in black, his favorite color. Yes, it was indeed Edward, Rebecca's brother. He was a distance from Rebecca but close enough to see the pain and yearning on her sad face as she watched Sharon and Phillip rode away. He spoke to himself. "Don't worry my dear sis, all this will become yours one day, you will see. You will get your sweet revenge that's my promise to you." As he spoke he walked backwards into the forest until the darkness consumed him and he was seen no more.

THE END

Printed in the United States
By Bookmasters